BEGINNINGS

An Australian Speculative Fiction Anthology

Various authors

Edited by Alanah Andrews,
Austin P. Sheehan & Jocelyn Spark

ISBN: 978-0-6484211-2-2

ABOUT THIS BOOK

'Beginnings' is an anthology featuring short stories
by 16 Australian Speculative Fiction authors.

The pieces are diverse explorations of the beginnings theme, told
through various genres; including sci-fi, fantasy, alternative history,
and paranormal.

http://www.aussiespeculativefiction.com

CONTENTS

Edge

Alanah Andrews

EACH MORNING AS THE sun peeked over the threshold of the world, Alma stood at the shore letting the colours wash blissfully over her body. First, the sky would seem just a little less dark. Then the stars would fade and a glorious display of crimson would creep over the horizon. Despite the fact that this was a daily occurrence, Alma never grew tired of observing the stunning mix of reds, pinks and oranges as they flowed like watercolour into her world.

She reached one hand up to her cheek, where a mark the colour of sunset stretched from her forehead, across her right eye, and onto her cheek. At first, Alma had felt self-conscious about the strange blemish on her skin, but her father had just smiled. "You've been touched by the sunrise, Alma," he had said. "You should be proud."

Alma smiled. But of course, she wasn't just there to see the sunrise. The reason she stood on the cool sand each morning was to gaze across the sea in wonderment at Edge as it grew gradually lighter in the rays of the sun. She could feel it calling to her.

Nobody else seemed to care about Edge, not like Alma.

Some of the villagers left, now and again, and paddled across the vast ocean, never to return. But they didn't seem to obsess over it as she did. They just woke up one morning, took one of the fishing boats and left with little fanfare. Or perhaps, she thought, Edge was always hovering at the back of their minds like it was for her, but they just never talked about it.

Alma often dreamed about Edge. She would be paddling towards it in a small canoe, leaving the safety of Island far behind. But every time she neared the brink of existence, the weather would turn, and the waves would rise like angry demons clawing and tearing at her small craft. Still, she wouldn't turn back, clinging onto the canoe and peering through the gigantic waves, hoping to catch a glimpse of what lay beyond.

Her dreams never allowed her to see what existed outside Edge—she would always wake up just as she got there, or be flipped out of the craft and sink quickly to the bottom of the ocean, hand outstretched in longing.

Father said she should be content with Island because it provided everything their community needed. They grew gardens full of vegetables. They prised abalone from the rocks and caught fresh fish each day. Dozens of coconut trees lined the shore, and a cool, clear, stream ran across the land and through their small village.

But despite the safety of Island, Alma felt trapped.

Each morning she would rush through her chores, then spend her time exploring every inch of Island while the other villagers worked in unhurried contentment. Her father would just shake his head, smiling.

"I've never met someone as curious as you, little Alma," he would say, his voice tinged with humour and exasperation.

Alma had explored from the top of the mountain where the small creek bubbled up from an underground spring, to the golden shores which ringed the land. There was no part of Island that Alma's feet had not yet touched. Edge was the only element in her life left unknown, and she longed to take one of those small fishing boats and leave like the others. Island made her feel safe. But Alma didn't always want to feel safe. She wanted to have answers.

Sometimes, while she was collecting food or fishing off the rocks, Alma would close her eyes and imagine standing in front of Edge. In reality, the sea would probably be too deep for such an act, but in her imagination it was shallow, and her feet would claw into the sand as the water rushed past her legs and down, down over Edge.

Into what? Where did the water go when it thundered over the precipice? Or was there a wall which contained the water and their world was simply a large, flat disk like the pebbles in the stream?

Her best friend, Ziel, hated it when she talked about Edge. "There's nothing beyond Island," he would tell her with firm certainty. "We have Island, Sea and Edge. That's it."

Alma gazed out at the sea which quietly lapped at the shore while they collected shellfish off the rocks. "How can there be nothing? I've seen plenty of people leave."

Ziel shrugged. "Sure, every now and then people are foolish enough to brave the waters. But they never come back. They either drown or fall off Edge into nothingness."

Alma wasn't so sure. "What if they found another Island?"

Ziel just smiled and shook his head. "If they found another Island then surely they would come back and tell us about it, right?"

Alma was forced to admit that the fact that the villagers never returned didn't bode well for life beyond Edge. She spent a long time gazing out at the waves, wondering, while Ziel dutifully filled the flax baskets with abalone for dinner.

"Where does the water go?"

"What?" asked Ziel absentmindedly as he inserted a thin stick beneath the large shell to prise it off the rock.

"The water," she repeated. "Where does the water go?"

"Over the Edge," said Ziel as though she had gone mad.

Alma thought for a while. "Edge is all around us, right?" she began, slowly. Ziel just ignored her and focused on his task, clearly wishing she would drop the subject. "So if the water is falling off Edge, then shouldn't the sea be getting shallower?"

"The water from the stream refills the sea," said Ziel firmly, confident that he had explained away her questions. "Now are you going to help me or not?"

Alma didn't ask again. It was true that the stream bubbled out of the spring, meandered lazily across Island and through the village, before entering the sea. But when Alma dreamed of Edge, the water rushing and plunging into nothingness was swift - far greater than the trickle of stream water.

Perhaps the rainwater fills it, she thought. Sometimes the rain pummelled down so heavily that it felt like there wasn't enough air between the droplets to breathe. Then the sky would roar, and the villagers would huddle together in their huts, waiting for the deluge to cease. But not Alma. The moment a storm began to brew she would be outside, waiting breathlessly for the flash of light and the ensuing rumble.

Alma decided to take her questions elsewhere.

"Father, is there a wall?" asked Alma.

Her father frowned. "What are you talking about?"

"At Edge. Is there a wall to hold the water in? Or does it just rush off Edge and fall... into what?"

"I don't know," he said at last. "Perhaps there's a wall, perhaps there's just Edge."

Alma was exasperated that nobody had any answers for her. "One day I'm going to paddle over there and find out."

Her father would just chuckle. "Perhaps one day you will," he said kindly, "but not today. Now do your chores."

Alma marvelled at the way the other villagers could be so blissfully ignorant about what lay beyond. She constantly felt Edge pressing against the inside of her mind, telling her to take a boat, to find out once and for all. But then Alma thought about Father, and about Ziel. She wasn't scared of Edge—well, perhaps a little bit—but she mostly didn't want to leave her friends and family if she could never return.

It was a warm, peaceful sort of day when Alma decided to explore the upper reaches of the river. She was skipping rocks across the smooth water when a log drifted lazily towards her in the current. She adjusted her aim, wondering if she could skip the rock right over the wayward branch without touching it. But as she lined it up in her sights, a disturbing thought crossed her mind. The bark was too smooth, the shape too strange for a log.

Without getting any closer she knew with calm certainty what it was.

The body was naked, and for a moment it felt like the time Ziel had fallen out of a tree while they were playing—part of her wanted to run away, but she knew she should help. For a brief moment, Alma considered letting it wash down the river and into the village to let her father deal with it. But no, that would be cowardly.

She knew it was dead. She had never seen a dead body, or known anyone who had died but somewhere in the recesses of her mind she knew it was true. It was face down in the water, with long, dark hair that fanned out like seaweed.

Steeling herself, Alma waded out into the shallows, grasped one pale wrist in her fingers and dragged the body to shore. Her skin crawled, but the body moved easily through the current and onto the land. She stared at the pale skin, wondering if she should try to flip the corpse over.

Suddenly, the body shuddered and convulsed like a freshly caught fish. Then it turned its head to the side and spewed clear liquid all over the ground. Alma leapt back with a scream.

When the strange, waterlogged girl finished throwing up the stream water, her bleary eyes turned towards Alma. "Where am I?" she asked croakily.

Alma found she couldn't answer, but the girl was shivering and Alma realised she must be terrified.

"Don't worry, I'll get Father," she called, sprinting off down the river to the village. She wasn't sure if she was running to get help or running to get away. Her heart hammered in her chest as she fought through the twisted vines and tree branches that seemed to be trying their hardest to slow her passage.

"Father!" she called loudly as she neared the village. "Father, come quick."

Father met Alma's panicked calls at the edge of the village, and between heaving breaths she quickly explained what she had found. But Father just nodded gravely. "It's fine, Alma. Just forget it—I will deal with her."

He turned away from Alma and marched towards their hut.

"Forget it?" said Alma in shock, hurrying to keep up with him. "No! Father, why was there a body in the river? Who is she?"

At the door of their hut, Father turned angrily towards her. "Why do you have to be so curious," he asked sternly. "Why? Everyone else is content, except for you."

Alma stuck her chin out in stubbornness, and her father rubbed one hand over his face. "I'm sorry. But if you didn't go exploring you would never have... Look... it's no major concern and you may as well know."

Alma stood silently, feeling excited despite the disturbing turn of events. She was going to get some answers. And then her belly clenched in fear, and she wondered if she really wanted to know. Father ushered her inside the hut, where he began rummaging through their belongings, looking for warm clothes and a blanket.

"The way that girl arrived? From River? That is also how you first arrived at Island. In fact, it's how we all came here. We arrive from River, then we stay on Island until we get *the call*. And then we leave."

Alma gaped, but there was no time to ask questions—Father had a pile of clothes in his arms and was already running upstream towards the girl.

Alma sat on the floor of the hut and thought about what he had said. She reached into the recesses of her mind, and realised that she had no recollection of being born. She couldn't remember being smaller or younger—it was as though she had always been this way.

But she couldn't remember arriving at Island either. How long had she been here? It seemed as though she had just opened her eyes one day and this was her existence. Was there something before Island? Were they birthed by the land?

There were too many unknowns, she decided. She needed to know the truth.

Without waiting for her father to come back, Alma sprinted down to the shore and dragged one of the canoes into the ocean. She knew that if she didn't do it now she would lose all resolve and probably never leave Island. Ziel, who was on the rocks fishing, saw what she was doing and raised his hand, palm open. Alma wasn't sure if he was telling her to stop or waving goodbye. She leapt into the small canoe, then raised one hand back at him in a fearful farewell.

As she plunged her paddle into the choppy seas, Alma glanced back over her shoulder. Some of the villagers were watching her leave, but many were simply continuing with their tasks. She knew that in a few minutes her father would arrive back at the village with the newcomer. Her eyes prickled with tears. Would the girl become his new daughter now that Alma had left? Was she making a terrible mistake?

But no, Edge was calling. She loved her community, and she did appreciate the safety that Island provided for her, but she refused to live in darkness any longer. She had to find out what lay beyond.

Alma focused all of her energy into digging her paddle deep into the water and pulling the canoe along. As she got closer and closer to Edge, Alma braced herself for the storm she was sure would unleash its fury upon her, like in her dreams. But it never came. The sea was calm, and slowly Island became smaller and smaller, until the people on the beach merged with the sand and palm trees.

After a while, Alma didn't need to paddle so hard anymore—the current dragged her swiftly along and away from Island. She felt a moment of panic in her chest—there was no turning back now.

She wondered if she would plunge off Edge like the waterfall crashing into the rocks on Island. Would she land amongst the stars? Or would her boat collide with some sort of enormous wall and she would be pinned against it by the current until she starved to death or drowned?

One minute she was paddling along, and the next, Edge was right in front of her. To her wonder, no waterfall appeared at all, and no solid barrier either. Instead, there was just a wall of pure white light.

Alma didn't feel scared anymore. As the light embraced her body, she closed her eyes, certain that this was what she was destined to do.

"JUST ONE MORE PUSH," said the woman dressed in white, and with a cry the newborn baby entered the world.

The nurse scooped the child up in her arms and checked her over. "You're an old soul," she murmured, placing the tiny child onto her mother's chest.

The baby's pale blue eyes looked around in astonishment. A mark the colour of sunset stretched across her face, from her forehead to her right cheek. The baby yawned widely and snuggled into her mother's embrace. As she fell into a blissful sleep, all memories of islands and edges faded, dissolved by the fluorescent glow of the hospital lights.

About the author

Alanah Andrews, like most humans, dislikes writing about herself in the third person. She shares regular snippets of random thoughts on http://www.facebook.com/alanahandrewsauthor and also has a website which occasionally gets updated: http://www.alanahandrews.com. She regularly has arguments with herself about whether 1984, Brave New World, or The Handmaid's Tale are most reminiscent of reality. You can download Alanah's novella 'The Harvest' for free from all retailers.

The Morrigan

Maddie Jensen

THE TIME FOR THE NEW Morrigan's ascent was at hand. Erin Brennan craned her neck to look up at the full moon, taking a steadying breath which misted out in front of her. This was the third Morrigan she had seen crowned in her nearly forty years, and she hoped it would be the last. The ceremony was important, but it was also not a pleasant process, and the latest chosen was the youngest in over a century.

The altar gleamed in the pale moonlight as Erin's gaze raked over the objects assembled; the ruby-hilted dagger, the silver box, and the ivory drinking horn. It had been almost twenty years since the last ascension ceremony, but many of the older witches still remembered the ritual.

A slight figure made her way through the assembly of witches toward the altar. Her hood was pulled over her head and a necklace of bones dangled around her neck. The sight made Erin's stomach tighten. As the cloaked figure reached the altar, she lowered her hood with trembling hands, her lips pressed into a determined line.

Cassidy Brennan, Erin's niece, was only seventeen years old—and the next Morrigan. After the brutal and sudden death of Erin's older sister Maeve, Cassidy had been the natural choice as her mother's successor. Though the bones she wore around her neck were her mother's fingers, Cassidy looked undaunted as she picked up the ivory drinking horn and the dagger, gazing around at the rest of the coven.

"To those who give their blood, I swear an oath of protection, and that I will serve the best interest of the coven at all times."

Cassidy turned to Erin. There had been some who had wondered whether Erin might challenge her niece for position of Morrigan, but it had never crossed her mind. Cassidy was young, younger than Maeve had been, yet she was very capable. Erin raised the dagger and slashed a deep cut across the palm of her hand, letting several drops of blood fall into the drinking horn before passing it on to the next witch.

Cassidy watched while the horn was passed around, brown skin gleaming in the full moon's light. Erin pitied her. The ritual was not a process for the faint of heart, and although she knew her niece was more than capable, Cassidy looked to her like a frightened girl. Once the horn had been passed around the coven, Erin handed it back to Cassidy, watching as she raised it to her lips without hesitation.

Maeve's death—along with the deaths of seven other witches and warlocks—had hit the coven hard. Yet none had been hit harder than Cassidy, still reeling from her recent loss. A trickle of the blood spilled from Cassidy's lips, down her chin and neck, but she made no move to wipe it away as she placed the horn and the dagger back on the altar.

Cassidy's eyes widened when she examined the silver box. They all knew what was concealed within. Cassidy looked to Erin, who gave her the slightest of nods. If becoming the Morrigan was easy, everyone would do it. Cassidy reached into the box and withdrew the item kept within. Several of the younger ones gasped, and one warlock looked away.

"Tonight, we honour the sacrifice of my mother and predecessor, Maeve." It had been Erin's job to teach Cassidy the words associated with the ritual, and the girl sounded almost robotic saying them. "I acknowledge my responsibilities as your Morrigan and beneath this watchful moon, I absorb the power of my predecessor."

Maeve's bloody heart rested in Cassidy's hands. Erin felt sick at the sight of it. Wearing her mother's bones was one thing, but what Cassidy had to do next was quite another. Yet the ritual must be completed for her to be recognised as the Morrigan, and to absorb the might of her predecessors. Erin folded her arms and watched Cassidy bring the heart to her lips. There was an awful crunch as she sank her teeth in.

Erin didn't look away while Cassidy consumed her mother's heart. This was what it meant to be the Morrigan. This was what it cost to absorb that kind of power. Every now and then Cassidy paused, but she never stopped. Erin smiled proudly. There had been whispers among the older witches that she wasn't ready, that she couldn't do it. Erin had always believed her niece would prove them wrong.

Cassidy sobbed as she finished the last of the heart, pushing it into her mouth and forcing herself to swallow. Her entire body convulsed, bloody fingers gripping the altar as she absorbed the power of the Morrigan. Her agonised scream ripped through the silent, watchful coven. For a few moments her eyes clouded over and went entirely white, a sign of her ascent. Erin had heard from Maeve that the pain of absorbing the Morrigan power was worse than childbirth.

With blood and gore streaming down her chin and tears running down her cheeks, Cassidy rose, pushing herself up from the altar.

A delighted smile spread across Erin's lips. "Our Morrigan rises."

Morrigan. The whisper went through the coven when they all kneeled before her. Cassidy sniffed, her entire body tense, but the coven's response coaxed a weak smile from her. She might be young, she might be scared, yet she was every bit her mother's daughter.

CASSIDY STOOD VIGILANT over her mother's grave, hands clasped in front of her to disguise the fact that her nails had bitten half-moon crescents into her palms. She knew who—or rather, *what*—had killed Maeve and the others. The whole coven did. They had some fancy government-sanctioned title, but the world of the supernatural knew them as The Hunt.

Their task was to bring down creatures who were doing harm or in danger of exposing the supernatural world to humanity. In this case, their job had been far more morally grey—Cassidy knew the coven would never have done anything to risk The Hunt's involvement.

"You're still thinking about it." A heavy hand on her shoulder, Erin's soft and melodic voice in her ear. "About what happened to them."

"How could any of us forget?" Cassidy's voice was bitter as she took in Maeve's name etched on the gravestone in front of her. "It wasn't right. It was violent and unnecessary. The Hunt's game has changed, and we still don't know why."

Cold wind whistled through the grave, but the two women stood steadfast. Cassidy reached up to place a hand over her aunt's. Erin's skin was smooth and soft to the touch. She had been the one to believe in Cassidy the most fiercely, the one who had convinced the coven that she had the mettle to become their next Morrigan despite her youth. She could never thank her aunt enough for that support.

Erin's hand tightened on her shoulder, before she withdrew it. Spinning around, Cassidy saw her aunt's icy gaze fixed upon a man crossing the graveyard, headed right for them. He was tall, dark-skinned and handsome. Cassidy had no idea who he was, but from Erin's expression, he wasn't good news. He offered the pair a benevolent smile as he reached the graves of their coven.

"Erin. You haven't aged a day."

"You are not welcome here." Erin spat, folding her arms over her chest. The sudden change in her gently-spoken aunt made a chill run up Cassidy's spine. Erin was a blood witch, and one drop was all it would take for her to make this man go running. Was he a member of The Hunt, or something worse still?

"Hi, Cassidy." He offered his hand for her to shake. "I'm Neal Rafferty. Your father."

Her stomach coiled unpleasantly, but she attempted to disguise any form of surprise. It was no coincidence, of that Cassidy was certain. Her estranged father showing up only days after her mum's death and her own ascension? Maeve had rarely spoken of the man, but when Erin had, it had been contemptuously. Part of the reason that Cassidy was so powerful for her age was Neal's blood running through her veins—the blood of a gancanagh. He'd seduced Maeve, their brief affair leading to her pregnancy with Cassidy.

Cassidy had seen few of the fair folk in her lifetime despite her biological connection with them, yet she knew they were dangerous. Their astounding beauty and warm smiles often disguised dark intentions and games of manipulation. Of all the supernatural creatures, it had been the fair folk that Maeve had warned her not to get involved with, most likely because of her own history.

"She doesn't want to see you," Erin hissed.

"She's old enough to decide for herself." Neal didn't even look at her, keeping his eyes on Cassidy. When she made no move to shake his outstretched hand, it dropped to his side. "I came because I heard about what happened to Maeve and I wanted to offer my condolences."

"You don't care about Maeve." Erin moved between Neal and Cassidy. "You don't care about Cassidy. You're here because you want something, so why don't you save us all some time and get to the point?"

Neal's brow furrowed. "I never got to know my own daughter because of Maeve, but that doesn't mean I never wanted to."

"Please just go." Cassidy's voice was tired and hoarse. She had no desire to see a showdown between Erin and Neal. She had come here to ruminate over the massacre, over her new role and what it meant for her. Neal's presence was sudden and unwelcome.

Neal stepped forward, leaning past Erin to press something into Cassidy's hand. She unfurled her fingers to see a business card with a mobile listed on it. She turned it over in her hands. So it looked like her father was working in accounting these days.

"In case you decide you do want to chat."

"She told you to go," Erin reminded him pointedly.

Neal offered her a humourless smile, putting his hands in the pockets of his coat and walking away. Cassidy watched him leave the graveyard with the feeling of something heavy sinking in the pit of her stomach. She didn't want anything to do with a man who she'd only seen a handful of times as a toddler—but what if Neal had answers? What if he knew more than he was letting on.

"You can't trust him, Cass," Erin insisted, taking her niece's hands in her own. "He'll play you like a fiddle."

Cassidy wrenched her hands away. She had never felt more lost and confused. The direct aftermath of the massacre had been a troubled peace, a sense that she knew what was to come, what her duty was. With Neal's sudden appearance, the balance had been thrown off course. There was only one solution, something that would ease her conflicted mind and set her on the right path.

Cassidy would consult the bones.

AMIDST THICK PLUMES of scented smoke, Cassidy sat cross-legged on the velvet throw rug and peered down at her findings. As a bone witch, like Maeve had been, she had an intuition for what the bones were trying to tell her. Closing her eyes and running her hand over the bones without touching them, Cassidy concentrated. The smell of frankincense was overwhelming, stinging at her eyes and making her feel like she might choke.

All was silent as she listened to what the bones had to say. She remembered Maeve teaching her the ways as a small child, as she'd squirmed around impatiently. It had come naturally to her, but she'd been fiercely competitive from a young age, wanting to be *better*. She had always known that she may be the Morrigan one day, but she'd never anticipated that it would be while she was still young, still in school.

Already the lines in her and Erin's relationship were blurred. The fact that her aunt was her legal guardian was complicated by the fact that Cassidy was the coven's Morrigan and therefore Erin's superior. Her aunt's protectiveness and understanding of Cassidy's authority had been apparent in their meeting with Neal. She wondered what Erin might have said if Cassidy had asked her father to stay.

It would have been easy for Erin to resent Cassidy. She was a grown woman, and there were some within the coven who said she should have replaced Maeve as the Morrigan after the massacre. Yet Erin had stepped aside and guided Cassidy instead. It couldn't have been easy, especially when many were apprehensive about a half-gancanagh Morrigan.

The bones remained oddly silent. It was as if there was something they didn't want to tell Cassidy. No matter how hard she listened, she couldn't gain any answers from them. Even when she opened her eyes and stared down at them, the thick smoke partially obscured them, their meaning unclear. Overcome by a wave of frustration, Cassidy gathered up the bones with impatient fingers, tossing them carelessly back into their satin bag.

The bones usually spoke freely to Cassidy, so this grim quiet unnerved her. If even the bones didn't have answers, then she was going to have to try different methods—methods that Erin wouldn't approve of. Withdrawing Neal's card from her pocket, she tapped the number into her phone and hit call.

CASSIDY JIGGLED HER legs nervously in the foyer at Rafferty Accounting. She hadn't expected her father to have his own firm. Waiting always made her apprehensive, and the plush leather seats and marble tiling did little to ease her nerves. She kept checking her phone, waiting for a message from Erin asking where she was.

The echo of clicking heels made Cassidy snap to attention, looking up to see Neal in a crisp black suit and dress shoes. There was amusement in his dark eyes—and he gave that warm smile that made her feel like they were close. Stuffing her phone into her handbag, Cassidy eased herself to her feet and followed him out of the foyer.

"I ... I'm sorry to disturb you. I didn't realise that this would be ... well ..."

"That I'd be in a well-established job with my own office?" Neal's voice was amused, his eyes mirthful as he ushered her into an empty room. "It's no trouble. I thought you'd call me eventually."

"The bones didn't tell me anything," Cassidy murmured, studying the folders on Neal's desk. She was ashamed of her inability to gain answers. As their new Morrigan, the coven was counting on her to avenge the deaths of those they'd lost to the massacre. They looked to her for leadership. She didn't feel that she was much of an inspirational figure at the moment.

"Ah, well, they wouldn't. There's a lot they probably don't want you to know."

Cassidy frowned. "What do you mean?"

Neal sighed heavily, leaning forward to rest his elbows on the desk and clasping his hands in front of him.

"You've only ever seen Maeve through the eyes of a daughter. Admiring eyes. But I know who she was when I met her, and what she was capable of."

Cassidy's eyes narrowed. "Just get to the point."

"I've only heard whispers." Neal leaned back in his chair, shrugging his shoulders. His dark eyes were fixed on his daughter. "But the vampires and the wolves are talking. The night of the massacre, your mum was planning something big. Something catastrophic. So, The Hunt put an end to it, before it could even begin."

"What sort of something?" The words were little more than a whisper, filled with dread.

"I know little of witches and warlocks, but I've heard of the power of hearts."

Cassidy's stomach twisted. It was well known that devouring hearts could bring a witch or warlock immense power. It was why the new Morrigan ate their predecessor's heart, provided it was still around. Hearts told stories. The consumption of hearts, other than for that sort of ritual, was strictly outlawed due to centuries of arguments on morality.

"So?"

"So, word has it that Maeve and some of the others wanted to move back into human sacrifice. Only those who deserved it, of course. But The Hunt took action once they realised your Morrigan planned on breaking the law."

"That isn't true," Cassidy protested, although in truth she couldn't have said for sure. Maeve and Erin had spoken on the merits of consuming animal hearts—a banned practice, but Maeve had always said that desperate times called for desperate measures. She had already broken the law on that count, although Cassidy doubted The Hunt would care for a few butchered animals. When it came to human lives, on the other hand ... the idea filled her with horror, but also fascination.

"I'm not saying she was a bad person." Neal held up his hands. "But The Hunt can be very black and white about these matters. If they caught wind of what your mum and the others were planning, they wouldn't have hesitated."

Cassidy sat there in stunned silence, the quiet broken by the sound of her ringtone shrilling through Neal's office. She fished it out of her bag, picking it up when she saw Erin's name on the screen.

"Hey."

"Where are you?" Erin's tone was panicked. She didn't even give Cassidy the opportunity to respond before she continued, her words fast-paced. "Never mind. You need to come to Desmond Shelby's, right now."

Cassidy's fingers tightened around her phone. Erin was always so calm, the voice of reason in a crisis. She'd helped Cassidy keep her cool in many a situation, so hearing her freaking out was enough to put Cassidy on edge.

"Why?"

There was a momentary pause. "Because he's dead."

CASSIDY MET ERIN AT the gruesome scene of the crime. Desmond Shelby had been a member of The Hunt—and an ally to the coven. After the massacre, he'd promised to look into it. She could remember him playfully flirting with Erin, who'd laughed off his attempts to ask her out in good humour. Now he was just a mangled corpse on a kitchen floor, his sightless grey eyes wide with terror.

Cassidy glanced at Erin. There were scarlet stains on her aunt's cheeks and chin, indicating that she had already tasted Desmond's blood to see what secrets it kept. Her expression, a mixture of sorrow and anger, told Cassidy all she needed to know.

"Oh, Des." Cassidy knelt beside his body, reaching over him to close his eyes. Had he found answers before his murder? Was that why he'd been killed so violently? Cassidy thought the punishment for betraying The Hunt would be severe. She jerked her head up to look at Erin. "What did you taste?"

"Fear, shock …" Erin shook her head slowly. "Nothing unexpected."

Swallowing the lump in her throat, Cassidy picked up the fallen knife that Desmond had likely used to defend himself. If the bones would not tell her the truth, his heart certainly would. The idea troubled and nauseated her, but she was starting to understand now, understand the choices that Maeve might have made.

She didn't know if Neal had been telling the truth. Yet Cassidy remembered the way Maeve's heart had tasted, the surge of power that had coursed through alongside the excruciating pain. She needed Desmond's heart to start this—her journey to retribution. There was no mistaking the irony in the situation as she raised the knife above Desmond's chest with shaking hands.

"What are you doing?" Erin asked.

"You should know." Cassidy looked hard in her direction. Her aunt looked away, and she realised that perhaps Neal had been right after all. That thought pushed her over the edge, gave her the resolve she needed to bring the knife down and carve out Desmond's heart. After several minutes of hard work, the knife dropped to the floor with a clatter, tossed aside as Cassidy observed her gory treasure.

"Cassidy." Erin's voice was choked, blue eyes wide and tearful. "If you do this, there's no going back. You can't know what consuming that will do to you."

"I do." Her eyes glinted as she held up Desmond's heart, warm blood oozing down her fingers. She raised the organ to her lips and, without hesitation, took her first bite.

At first everything was a blur, spinning fast enough to make her feel sick. Cassidy was new to this, so she forced the rush of Desmond's memories to slow and clear, picking through until she found exactly what she wanted. Desmond's killer wasn't another member of The Hunt. It wasn't even a witch or warlock. The remains of his mutilated heart fell from Cassidy's fingers as she shook with indignation.

"Cassidy?" Erin's voice was soft, and it was only when Cassidy really set eyes on her aunt that she realised the woman was frightened. Frightened *of her*. Of the creature she might become in her quest for truth and justice. But was this just about answers now?

"It was the gancanagh." Her voice was hollow. How could she have been so foolish? Erin had warned her, yet she hadn't listened. "It was Neal."

Had her father played a role in her mother's death? Was he allied with The Hunt? Was The Hunt even responsible for the massacre? Cassidy's head pounded as she tried to process the unanswered questions.

"Ready the coven." Cassidy picked up a tea towel, wiping blood and gore from her hands. "The Hunt may still have been involved with this. Other supernatural creatures might have been too. We'll have any heart we require for the real story to come to light."

Something devious lit up Erin's face. "But, the law..."

Desmond's heart was a start, but it wasn't enough. Was it the gancanagh or the witch in her that craved more power? Was it both? The taste of hearts was slowly becoming addictive, as well as the benefits that consuming them brought. She would have more until she had the heart that would be her last—Neal's.

"I am your Morrigan." The words were cold as the wind that had whipped through the graveyard the day Cassidy had met her father. "I am the law now."

About the author

Maddie Jensen is a Sydney author who has been writing from a very young age. Majoring in Journalism at Curtin University, Maddie predominantly writes science fiction and fantasy. Follow her on Instagram at maddiejensenwriter

The Vessel

Matthew P. Copping

MORNING SUNLIGHT FILTERED through the curtained window. A beam caressed Maggie's face and she stirred. Her head pounded and a dryness filled her mouth.

Blinking the weight from her eyelids, she processed what she could see. A white dress lay at the foot of her bed. Folded as it was, she could make out the blossoms embroidered into the lower bodice. Atop sat a locket of carved wood, worked into the shape of an oak tree; its branches and roots curved and weaved, forming concentric rings around the trunk and leaves.

Maggie shifted upright, dangling her feet over the edge of the bed. As if they had been waiting, two acolytes entered the room and assisted her in getting dressed. They pulled the dress over Maggie's head, threading her hand carefully through the laced left arm. The intricate pattern of leaf and blossom fit perfectly along the length of her arm, anchoring to a ring sewn into the fabric.

"Is she getting...?" Maggie left the question unfinished, as one of the acolytes left the room. The second acolyte started combing the thicket atop Maggie's head, offering a small smile in response. Finally, content with her efforts, she moved in front of Maggie, the locket in hand. She held the band wide, placing it over Maggie's head without messing up her hair again.

"Grandmother used to tell me stories of when she had been chosen, but I never thought it would be so..."

"It is a great honour to be chosen," the acolyte said, before offering a sheepish smile and a small bob of her head.

Before Maggie could strike up any further conversation, the acolyte returned with an ornate wooden box. Maggie swallowed the lump growing in her throat and hesitated before accepting the offered box. She admired the intricately carved oak that held her grandmother's ashes, running her fingers along the design. She took a deep breath to steel herself against the tears threatening to fall. The acolytes continued to prepare Maggie for the ceremony, adding blossoms to her hair and makeup to her face. She closed her eyes and settled back, letting the memories of the previous few days filter through her mind.

THE FIGURE LYING UPON the bier barely resembled the woman Maggie knew; even the familiar smell had an acidic tinge to it. Those strong limbs that had carried Maggie up the nearby mountains as a child, had now diminished into sagging skin, barely covering bone. Her olive complexion was spotted and marred with dark blotches of bruising like forgotten fruit.

Maggie tore her eyes away from her grandmother's body, tears falling freely as she glanced around the linen walls of The Vigil. In keeping with tradition, it had been built by the departed's loved ones. Maggie admired the paintings, suspended from The Vigil's wooden supports, representing her grandmother's finest moments. Carved statuettes and woven baskets, full of fruit and flowers, adorned a large table at the far end of the tent; gifts from the village celebrating Elizabeth's life.

I remember this one, Maggie thought, lifting a painting to take a closer look. Her grandmother, as a child, stood next to two girls who would become First and Second of Seven. Elizabeth had never risen to rank, yet she led the children in this painting. A wolf crouched low—threatening—whilst the girls played along a river scene. Elizabeth was painted between the wolf and the future leaders of her village; protecting who, from what, was uncertain.

"She was always a kind woman," a gravelly voice called from the entrance of the tent. "I *am* sorry for your loss."

Maggie jumped, dropping the painting. Raking her fingers through her dishevelled hair in an attempt to make herself presentable, she spun around. Bowing low, she placed fingertip to forehead, as was customary within the mountain tribe. She remained in her pose, left knee to the dirt ground and head lowered, as the newcomer inspected the tributes.

"Do you know why you are here, child?" Ivy asked, coming to stand before Maggie. She crouched and cupped Maggie's chin, forcing Maggie to meet the First of Seven's gaze.

"I am to be Grandmother's chosen," Maggie replied. *If the ancestors accept me.*

Ivy picked up the painting from the dirt beside Maggie, dusting off the frame before hanging it back up. "That was a lifetime ago, well before I became the First. And look—there's Kira.

She was destined to be Second of Seven since well before that day. As soon as the wolf limped to the river, she'd wanted us to fight. 'Chase it off to protect the village!' she had shouted."

The First of Seven made her way to Elizabeth's body and placed a delicate kiss against her forehead.

"Your grandmother always had the largest heart of all of us. She planted herself between Kira and the wolf, demanding we help it instead." Ivy shook her head in wonder. "Help a wolf? But help we did. Something in the way she sang to it as she approached calmed the beast and we managed to wash its wound and let it go free.

"She was never meant for the Seven, your grandmother. We are protectors of *our* people. Kira was right back then—a wolf is a menace to our people. That is why she is a great Second. Isabella weaves her magic and keeps us safe from the spiritual as the Third. The others are dedicated to the safeguarding of our beliefs and dedications. They offer themselves to the elements so we may be safe within our grove." Ivy crouched low before Maggie and placed a palm against her face.

"We need people like Elizabeth; people who choose what is right, over their self-interests."

Ivy made her way over to the assorted offerings, picking up several pieces and replacing them. Her hands moved slowly and carefully. "Do you remember your lessons?"

Maggie nodded her head in response. All children of the People of the Seven were taught from a young age about the chosen and the rituals. "It is the way of our people. To honour the Mother of All and complete the cycle."

"That's right." Ivy nodded. "Centuries ago, before the Great War swept the land, we knew nothing about the Mother. As the war raged on, our people became ... lost ... intoxicated with their fight. It afflicted our men worse; each and every one became infatuated with the violence until none remained.

"Our people, faced with our own reckoning, were torn apart. The original Seven fled with what few women remained. They wandered the lands, searching for peace and safety, and eventually the Mother presented herself to them. Ever since, the Mother has sustained us. She gives us food, shelter and life. That is why you have been chosen. This village needs people with Elizabeth's heart."

The First of Seven turned to depart, pausing to offer a final thought. "Take care during the ritual. Keep the Great Oak in your thoughts and let its presence root you here ... in this reality."

"... READY?" THE ACOLYTE's voice broke through her memories, a concerned expression on her face. "Chosen one? Are you ready?"

"I'm ready," Maggie announced, her voice calm and steady, much to her surprise.

The acolytes led Maggie along a cobble-stone pathway to the grove of the Great Oak. Mourners lined the path, offering prayers and consolation. Maggie remembered having been amongst the crowd in the past, offering her own best wishes to the chosen. She focused on the rough stones of the path pressing into her bare feet.

The trail forked to either side as it reached the grove, encircling the Great Oak and joining back together on the opposite side of the giant tree. Before her, as the stone path split, petals lay strewn upon the grass leading into the grove. Maggie knew it had been the Third of Seven herself who had scattered these petals upon the sacred ground. The acolytes stopped at the path's edge and urged her forward onto the green.

Maggie stepped barefoot on to the grass and cheers arose from the village people lining the stone path. She continued along the trail of petals, snaking around the oak to end at the front of the grove, before the village centre. She stopped at the end of the floral track in front of Isabella, the Third of Seven. A welcoming smile adorned the elder's face, yet never reaching her vacant eyes—the Third stood partway between realities, part within the physical realm and part within the spiritual.

"Welcome, my child," Isabella rasped. The simplicity with which she spoke seemed at odds with the pomp and fanfare surrounding Maggie. The villagers were well into the celebration of her grandmother's life and the arrival of the chosen had elevated them into a cacophony of merriment and festivity, but the words of their Third brought silence to the celebration. "Kneel."

Maggie obeyed. Moisture leaked through her thin white dress as her knees pressed into the soft ground. The giant oak overhead, with its multitude of branches overlapping each other, offered protection from elements, both sun and rain; however, the early morning dew, normal for this time of year, kept the grove luscious and damp without the heat of the sun.

"Do not be sad," the Third said, as she slowly walked around Maggie. "We will all keep Elizabeth's memory alive ... here." She tapped Maggie's chest lightly with the butt of her staff. Isabella leaned in close and whispered into Maggie's ear. "But I do miss my old friend dearly."

Returning her attention to the assembled crowd, she continued her oration. "This day, we honour and celebrate a dearly loved member of our tribe. This day we say farewell." Isabella planted her staff into the soft ground.

"Mother of All, welcome our friend into your embrace!" The Third of Seven swung her staff around, giving the oak a sharp rap on its trunk. A deep *thud* echoed out, resounding from the leaves of the Great Oak themselves. The echoing sound reverberated and multiplied, intensifying in sound and pitch until a lone acorn dropped to the grove floor, a foot in front of Maggie.

Opening her arms out wide, Isabella welcomed the gathered people onto the grove. The villagers stepped onto the sacred ground, encircling Maggie and the Third in a ring of exuberance. Maggie inched forward toward the acorn and scooped up layers of dirt and grass from the moist forest floor.

Shaking, Maggie raised the ornate box above her head and cast her eyes about the gathered crowd. She locked eyes with Isabella, who gave her an encouraging nod of the head.

"Farewell and welcome," Maggie sung out, emptying the contents of the box into the hole.

"Farewell and welcome!" the crowd echoed in kind, breaking into applause.

Maggie scooped the dirt forward over the hole, burying her grandmother's ashes beneath the Great Oak.

Isabella's staff planted into the ground again, cutting the crowd's jubilation off as her otherworldly eyes cast around the collective.

"I give you ... the vessel!" The roar erupting from the crowd was louder than the summer thunders and the celebration began anew.

Isabella knelt before Maggie, the stone ritual bowl in hand. Into the dish the Third of Seven placed the acorn from the Great Oak and began grinding the nut into a fine dust with a pestle. Once satisfied, she produced a leather wine-skin from beneath her voluminous robes and poured a dark liquid into the bowl. She stirred the contents into a thin paste before offering the mixture to Maggie.

"Drink, Vessel. And may the ancestors bless you."

Maggie drank deeply, the mixture bitter on her tongue. The paste acted quickly and Maggie closed her eyes against the uncontrollable spinning. Her body felt heavy and she was thankful she already knelt on the ground, lest she collapse. Still, she slowly walked her hands backward to lay beneath the great oak, jubilation from the crowd echoing against the canopy above.

"Don't tarry, my child," Isabella's voice whispered into her ear, cutting through the gradually strengthening hum. "Lest they not allow your return."

MAGGIE WOKE UP AMONGST darkness. She found herself on a small island, a refuge in an ocean of nothingness. The void beyond the coastline was complete, endless blackness. Before her, a bridge spanned the void to a second, slightly larger island. Torches burned brightly from the centre of it and Maggie could make out figures dancing.

Crossing the bridge toward the light, Maggie hugged her arms tightly to her body against the creeping cold. Time moved at an odd pace, each step slow and difficult, as though underwater. Maggie struggled across the bridge, Isabella's words of warning ringing in her ear.

Finally, she stepped foot on the far island, the torches offering some small measure of warmth. She found herself in the midst of a small festival. Tables stood in the centre of the island, lined with platters of meats and fruit. Ignoring the tables, dancers pranced and pirouetted past Maggie, their grins plastered from ear to ear and soundless laughter on their lips.

"The ancestors welcome Elizabeth," a voice said from behind Maggie. "Why should we send her back?"

The voice pulled at Maggie's soul, as only a God's could. In those few words, Maggie wanted to embrace the Mother of All, but in the same breath, she wanted to run from her. Maggie edged toward the banquet, suddenly ravenous, the voices urging her forward to eat.

Maggie blinked away the beckoning food and turned to face a beautiful woman, her pale skin contrasted by the dark green of the vines wrapping around her lithe body. Her eyes were a deep brown and Maggie could see the torch-light reflected within them, dancing in the non-existing wind—beside her stood Maggie's Grandmother. Strength had been returned to her amongst the spirits of her ancestors.

Maggie knelt before the pair, bowing her head. The woman reached forward and placed a hand on Maggie's forehead. The air exploded from Maggie's lungs as a wave of memories flashed before her eyes.

Barely visible amongst the onslaught, the ancestors gathered about the prostrate Maggie; whispers echoed in her ears, incomprehensible, but holding with them a sense of judgement. The murmuring intensified as the memories flickered. Each vision accompanied by a pulsing emotion radiating from the crowd surrounding her.

Maggie was a child play wrestling with some of the other children. She knew she shouldn't be wearing the robe, but was swept up in the drama. She played the part of an exotic warrior, arriving from far away to battle for matters of the heart. Rose played the Second of Seven, the protector of the village.

Rose was always a fierce competitor. She took the role of Second seriously, as though she herself had been tasked with the protection of the tribe.

Maggie tackled Rose and for once seemed to have the upper hand. She managed to pin her to the ground by the collar. Forgetting her role as the travelling warrior, Maggie shouted glories to the ancestors above. Revelling in her apparent victory, she did not notice Rose's arm snaking inside her robe.

A subtle shift of Rose's hips below her brought Maggie back to the wrestle, but too late to combat the oncoming move. In one swift motion, Rose shifted Maggie's arm aside and shot her left leg behind her neck. Rose settled slowly backward, the fire building inside Maggie's arm until she almost screamed out in pain.

"Is she worthy?" the whispers questioned.

The question pulled at Maggie; a sharp tug with the promise of eternal oblivion. A cold settled into her fingertips.

"Careless ..." came a reply, the voice weightless and airy.

"Irresponsible," another agreed.

The cold crept up her arms.

"No ... honest."

Maggie was now fifteen. Her hands hurt. She glanced down at the burning sensation and saw blood seeping from dozens of scrapes and bruises. Still, she worked at the flax-leaves. The leaves slipped in the blood as she tore long strips. Her fingers moved quickly, despite the slickness and pain, interlocking the new piece amongst the others. She continued weaving the strands, working tirelessly throughout the night.

"Yes," breathed the collective surrounding her.

The memory flickered again; it was now dawn. Maggie stood with the other villagers, offering her woven rug to a for-lorn-looking family. She could smell the soot and ash on their clothes.

"Selfless," the voices returned. The whisper held a hint of sat-isfaction to it.

Warmth returned to Maggie's fingers as the next vision en-veloped her.

Maggie wiped the fresh tears from her cheeks and settled in-to preparing her grandmother's body for the afterlife. She un-tied the sash bound at Elizabeth's waist, allowing the sides of her robe to fall away. Maggie choked at the sight of her grandmoth-er's naked body, gaunt as it had now become.

Moving a small table, Maggie carefully positioned it behind the bier, away from any draft that might enter The Vigil. She opened the leather pouch and carefully removed the ritual items onto the table; a candle, thick and tall, scented with acorn and mountain pepper-berry; a shallow and wide bowl, carved out of a green, speckled river-stone; an ivory figurine of a lady, garbed in a dress of flowering vine, its tendrils clinging tightly to the figurine's body; a sharp knife.

Maggie unclasped the locket from Elizabeth's neck and curled the jewellery around the base of the candle. She breathed deeply, steeling herself against the moments to come. *This is it. May the ancestors bless me.*

"Mother of all, hear our wishes." Maggie reached for the ivory statuette, clutching it to her chest. She leaned forward and gently blew on the candle wick. A flame sprang to life, spreading a peppercorn-and-acorn scent throughout The Vigil.

Maggie shivered as the tent became cold. Whispers nipped at the back of her mind, beckoning.

Stay anchored. The thought settled Maggie. Many chosen had been lost to the pull of the ancestors in the past. *I am the Great Oak.*

She plunged the cloth into a bucket of water, sending a floral fragrance into the air to intermingle with the candle. The combination smelled of a spring morning in the nearby grove.

"Might the rain wash away the pains she has endured and nourish the joys, so she may know joy eternal," she said, wiping her grandmother's forehead and cheeks gently with the perfumed water. *I am the leaves amongst the canopy. I bathe in the torrent.*

"Might the wind spread the love she has felt far and wide, so she may know love eternal." The cloth pressed against Elizabeth's bosom and stomach. *I am the branches and bark. I bend with the breeze.*

Maggie breathed deeply and dipped the cloth into the bucket again, wringing the excess water out.

"Might fire burn away the ailments of her body, returning the strength of her youth, so she may know strength eternal." Maggie cleansed the arms. *I am the trunk. I am renewed amongst the inferno.*

"Might the earth forever nurture her accomplishments, so she may know pride eternal," Maggie spoke the words, as she washed the legs and feet. *I am the roots. The anchor within the ground.*

"These words I offer to you and the ancestors, so they might welcome her into their arms. These words I offer to you and the ancestors, so we might keep her in our hearts. These words I offer to you and the ancestors, so they might aid her in the return." Maggie reached out for the bowl of dirt beside her Grandmother. Taking the knife from the table, she drew a small cut across her wrist, the blood dripping into the bowl. *I am the Great Oak. I know my place. I stand strong.*

"Mother of all, bear witness," Maggie said, bowl outstretched above her head. She held her breath and brought the bowl toward the candle. Carefully, she poured the dirt onto the candle, smothering the flame, barely a wisp of smoke escaping.

The cleansing completed, Maggie sunk to her knees. Her shoulders slumped as the exhaustion settled in and she began to tremble. The words raced back through her mind, replaying them again and again.

"Respect ..." the voices murmured.

Warmth spread throughout Maggie's body.

Maggie was on the island again, hunched over on hands and knees, gasping for air. Her Grandmother stepped forward, offering her hands to help Maggie to her feet. She smiled deeply, placing a hand to Maggie's stomach before kissing her forehead.

MAGGIE AWOKE BENEATH the Great Oak. The crowd had dispersed and she found herself alone on the grass with a humming Isabella. The Third of Seven was busy with her needle, threading away at a silk piece of material.

"And such is the way of the Women of the Seven. The spirits of our ancestors live on through the chosen—should they be deemed worthy," Isabella said, her hands gesturing around her at the newly grown daffodils.

With Isabella's help, Maggie stood. A wave of nausea threatened to seat her again, sending her hand to her stomach to try to calm the churning. Isabella held out the silk material she had been working on—Maggie's Grandmother's robe had been altered into a blanket.

"The daffodil is nature's symbol of rebirth. The circle continues," the Third of Seven explained. "You're—"

Maggie cut Isabella off. "I'm pregnant!"

About the author

Matthew P. Copping lives with his head amongst the clouds. His favourite pastime is buying small versions of food and pretending he is a giant. When he is not enjoying the little things in life, he is an author, parent, husband and banker. He lives in Launceston, Tasmania with his wife, daughter, two dogs, a cat, and his entourage of imaginary friends. Matthew decided to pursue his writing career early 2018 and is excited to have his first short story published. You can follow his writing at https://www.facebook.com/runicrumblings

The Inheritance Experiment

Kel E Fox

BRNO, AUSTRIAN EMPIRE: 1899

Esmerelda did not remember much of the year she turned three, even though she had perfect recall of every year since. What she did remember from that year was a dream. She was in her mama's garden, picking cream-and-yellow jonquils to put in her favourite vase, the pretty blue one. Like most of her dreams, it was fuzzy around the edges. Esmerelda was squatting in the rich black soil of the garden bed, feeling the dirt shift between her toes and reaching to touch the tip of a delicate yellow petal, gently, so it wouldn't be broken. She didn't see her mama so much as know she was there.

At least, she thought it was her mama.

"Ezzie!"

It was time to go back inside. Esmerelda felt the chilly wind against her face, the deep cold of the earth rising up through her bare feet, but she herself wasn't cold. Besides, this was a dream, so she could stay out in the garden as long as she liked. In her

41

dream, the sun didn't even have to go behind the clouds. Mama said she was special because of the way she could control dreams. So young, Mama said, for such a thing. She already knew more than all the other children in Sunday School. Even Abbot Johann was impressed.

"Ezzie!" Louder this time, and she felt Mama approach in that dream-like way when she knew something was happening without knowing how. It was just so. Mama's shoes clopped on the path as she walked up behind Esmerelda.

The woman she thought was Mama put rough arms around the chubby little girl with blonde pigtails and swept her out of the garden just as the girl realised it wasn't Mama. It was a man, and something was wrong because Papa was away—again she knew this in the dream, it was just so. Mama wasn't there at all now.

Esmerelda didn't have a chance to gather herself and make the dream hers again. The stranger trampled over the jonquils and carried her away with her face pointing at the ground so all she could see was the stones of the footpath until it was the steps of a carriage. She knew she must fight. Her limbs were not working, though. They were too heavy. She willed them to fight, to bite and kick and scream, but her voice was gone too. A small part of her said it's okay, it's a dream, it's a nightmare, they come sometimes and when it gets too bad you'll wake up and Mama and Papa will be there with hugs and kisses and maybe they'll let you sleep in their bed for the night. She gave up on her unwilling body, allowing it to be thrust into the windowless carriage. She lay in the darkness, alone, waiting to wake up.

She didn't wake up.

She dreamed of darkness, endless darkness, with no way to bring the sun back or change the story to a good one the way she sometimes did. She thought it might be painful to dream of darkness, but she didn't feel anything. Even when she dreamed that a thousand needles marched over her during the night, pricking her skin, she didn't feel anything. The needles turned into knives, and still she didn't feel anything, nothing but blackness like a weight, pressing into her being. When she saw the faces looming in the dark, so close to hers, she found her voice. *Good*, she thought with the tiny part of her that still could think. *You always wake up when you scream.*

They pushed her off a cliff. She watched the jagged rocks below approach in slow motion. She was calm because no matter how bad a nightmare got—and sometimes they could be really bad like this—she would always wake up just before she died.

Esmerelda hit the ground and felt her body break into a million pieces.

She woke up the year she turned seven. She had dreamed for four years. Her body felt odd, too big, her fingers long and thin and her cheekbones stood out in her face when she saw her reflection. She remembered every moment, but it wasn't real. She wondered if she had somehow jumped ahead in time, and she only had the memory of those four years. But there was something wrong with the memories. She had no family in those memories. She squeezed her eyes shut, willing her brain to find the tram rides to the markets with Mama, or breakfasts at the table with Papa reading the paper before he went to work. Those things must have happened, but the memories weren't there. Where she should have been sharing dinner in the warmth of her home, she was eating cold food alone in the dark room they said was hers, even though it didn't have the patchwork quilt Mama made or her woolly teddy bear. She had lived through hours and days and months of darkness. Her mind scrabbled fruitlessly after an explanation.

Eventually she realised she had been awake all along, in the dark room. It wasn't a dream. And she should have died, but she hadn't.

THE NEXT TIME ESMERELDA had control of her thoughts, she was fifteen. She had observed another three thousand days of her abduction and darkness, years of darkness, with no control over anything. Not her body, nor her mind. Every moment had a space in her memory, except nothing had happened. Just darkness. Or ... maybe there was more, behind the darkness. Cold food. Fuzzy lights and needles and syringes and men with whispering voices who reminded her of the abbots at church. If she focused, she could remember other things, painful things, things like falling off cliffs, blue electric fire torching her veins, sharp knives releasing her blood to the floor, drowning in salt water. The electrocution had been first, though. It was better not to look too closely, but Esmerelda was fairly certain she had died, or should have died, at least five times. Even when she'd dreamed of sleeping, she couldn't escape from the relentless recording of time and memory.

When she was fifteen, the men in robes asked her to kill a rabbit. It was sitting in front of her, sweet and trusting, twitching its pink nose. The white fur was soft under her fingers as she picked it up and twisted its neck as if it were a bread stick. That was when her mind snapped into focus. She hadn't done this before. She looked at the men standing around her with their notepads, nodding to each other and talking excitedly. The rabbit was limp in her hands as she lay it back on the table. She felt how strong her fingers were, how she could have crushed its tiny fragile body to pulp if she'd wanted to. What she wanted was to yell, scream, do something to show how wrong this was, but her voice would not obey her commands. When one of the men took her by the elbow to lead her back to her room, she couldn't make her arm hit him in the face.

Just after she turned seventeen, they sent her to assassinate an archduke. She had no idea who he was or why she was doing it, but she was so strong and so fast it was easy. Someone else was caught for her crime. After that, it was just blood. They—the abbots, she realised as they left the church she'd been imprisoned under—cut her hair to look like a boy, instructed her to bind her chest and she became Kadett Bischoff. At first, some of the soldiers were suspicious, but most couldn't believe that a woman could be so physically strong. And she wasn't alone. Bischoff found Kadett Krenn washing her bloodied underwear in a hidden pool. They joked that in a war as bloody as this, it would be a little blood that would give them away.

The hardest thing was the noise. Bischoff's senses were especially sharp since leaving the quiet confines of the church, and the gunfire blast was just the start. She could hear the sounds of the bullets ripping through muscle, smashing bones, tearing through organs. It was different again with brains. The stench was almost enough to knock her out long before the other soldiers began complaining. At least in the taste department, she could be thankful for their bland rations.

By the end of the first year, no one bothered with suspicions. Any lucky bastard with a gun was man enough, and Bischoff was the luckiest bastard of them all. She got promoted to *Stabsfeldwebel* purely because she was still alive at the end of every battle, and she promoted Krenn as high as she could manage to keep her close. Bischoff followed orders, gave orders, and when she received a visit from an abbot, she would do what they ordered too. Her mind cried out questions. Her voice would just say yes to whatever they asked.

Krenn died in Bischoff's arms in 1918. Bischoff didn't think. She usually thought: *I won't do this, I won't fire.* Then she'd fire anyway, because her body didn't do what her mind asked—it did what the men in robes had told her to do. Another man would fall, stumbling to his knees, falling into the bloody mud, never to return to his home. And Bischoff would think: *Next time. Next time I'll be stronger.* When Krenn fell, Bischoff didn't think. In the middle of the charge, the Stabsfeldwebel threw her rifle down and dropped to the ground beside the other woman. Her men surged past, thinking Bischoff another fallen comrade. Rank didn't matter once you were dead, at least not until they stopped to count the fallen. Bullets were flinging into Bischoff's chest and back, puncturing her liver and lungs and she even felt one tear her gallbladder apart, but none of that mattered either. She felt the life leave her best friend in all the world and her heart howled. In the blood and mud and shrapnel of the battlefield, Bischoff felt something snap, and it wasn't physical. She looked at the gun. Her body was already healing, even as new pellets smashed through her skin. She was supposed to pick up her gun. She was supposed to go on, fighting, shooting, killing. She almost did it, but her mind was stronger now. Bischoff lay down in the mud and let her grief take over instead.

She should have known they would find her. She broke the nose of the abbot who came for her in the makeshift hospital on the edge of the war zone. The nurses smiled sympathetically, murmuring about the shock and how it would pass, and it was a miracle she'd survived without even a scratch. The abbot blocked the nurses' view with his robed body as he slipped the needle into Bischoff's arm. She sank back into the dark dream.

BISCHOFF WAS IN HER room, featureless but familiar. Only now she was truly awake, she didn't think of it as a room. It was a cell. She knew it had only been a few weeks since the ... since Kre— ... since the battlefield. She had counted the days. They electrocuted her again. When it seemed to have not had the desired effect, they did it again, and again, and finally they left her burning in the blue current for fifty-three hours, twelve minutes and twenty-five seconds. She felt herself grow stronger. There were long sessions of drugged hypnosis. Then they had subjected her to extremes: explosive noises that tore her ear drums to miniscule shreds, only for them to instantly heal and tear again. Strobe lights that burned her retinas and made her see monsters in the shadows for a week after, and smells that she couldn't identify but which had made the bloodied, rotten battlefields almost jasmine. At first, each sensory overload was unbearable. She wished she would die. But she slowly learned to shut the input out, turn the volume down, not allow her brain to take in so much information that it was painful even to think. Finally, after she had managed to not react to the paste concentrate they had forced into her mouth—twenty-two varieties of strong herbs and four types of pepper she identified in a detached part of her mind—they had left her in her cell for a whole nine hours. Just to sleep, even on the lumpy mattress provided, might have been nice. Bischoff couldn't remember what nice was. There were so many things she wished she could forget, but she couldn't remember what nice was. She sighed. A cry escaped her mouth; she turned it into a choked cough.

"Ezzie?" The voice was impossible. There was a small window on each side of her cell, more of a vent, too high to see through. But the voice was enough. Bischoff hadn't forgotten.

"Mama," she whispered. With her hearing now, she could hear the abbots working and muttering several floors above. They would not hear any talking, but Bischoff wanted quiet more than anything, just about. Mama would hear her through the window.

"Oh, Ezzie. I thought, when they took you, that you had ..."

"What are you doing here, Mama?"

"Why, the same as you. The inheritance experiment. They are trying to make us like gods, Ezzie."

Bischoff's first thought was that Mama had signed them up for this. But she made herself listen to the broken voice again. She could hear more than just sounds now: when someone spoke, she knew things about them, somehow. She heard pain in her mother's voice, and fear, and guilt over not protecting her baby girl. A loss of faith in her belief. But most of all, she heard the resignation of a dying woman.

"What have they done to you?" Bischoff asked, ignoring the hot wet tear sliding down her cheek.

"It didn't work for me. There's nothing more they can do now." Almost relief. "But it worked on you. I heard them talking. They are very excited about you."

Bischoff felt rage build in the pit of her being, roiling, scrabbling at her soul. Eventually, she tamed it enough to ask, "what happened to Papa?"

"They took him too." Mama's voice broke. "You have to get away from here, Ezzie. However long it takes. You can't die now. You are stronger than they are. You can do it."

"I will get you out," Bischoff muttered, climbing to her feet. She could just break the door down. She was strong enough, and she didn't know why it hadn't occurred to her before. A worm of an idea slipped through her mind, like gripping at air. There was a reason it hadn't occurred to her. She couldn't grasp what it was. No matter. She let her rage rise, preparing to unleash it upon the door—

"Wait."

Bischoff stopped mid-flight.

"It's too late for me," Mama continued, "but you need to plan. If you break the door down now, they'll catch you and chain you and drug you and you'll never get out. You need to time it, and strike at your best chance."

"I can't let you die in here alone." There was that crack in her voice again. She willed herself to be strong.

"You must, Ezzie. Let me at least do this much for you. Plan your escape, my clever, brilliant girl. If you get out, my death will be worth it. In the long run." Mama's voice faded. Bischoff could hear her breathing, shallow and rasping.

There was nothing more to say. Bischoff sat with her back against the stone wall and listened to her mother die in silence while she nursed her anger, honing it to a sharp, controlled point.

That night she dreamed properly for the first time in two decades. She dreamed of Krenn. Halfway through, Bischoff became lucid. She was grateful for the increased accuracy of her memory: this dream didn't have fuzzy edges. Antonia Krenn's face was hard, but only because of the grimace she always wore to stop people speaking to her. Her soft green eyes gave her away; to Bischoff, at least. Krenn had kept her hair short since before the war, helping her brothers on the family farm and disappointing her parents with her refusal to marry. She had joined the army to follow her brother. Bischoff remembered this as she simply sat and gazed at the other woman, older than Bischoff but shorter and slighter and far more fragile. Bischoff woke with a vow to avenge Krenn, somehow. Someone had to pay for the war. And find out what had happened to Krenn's brother. The dream reawakened the knowledge she'd found as Krenn died on the battlefield: there was a link between her and the abbots that controlled her, but she could break it. She could escape.

They had more needles for her the next day, and more drugs. This time she fought the torpor and the unrelenting pressure to just let go of her body, view it all from the detached corner of her mind where she experienced her life as a waking dream. The two abbots attending her cottoned on though.

"She's developed a resistance. Look at her pupils."

"So she has. Up the dosage then."

They pumped another syringe into her veins. Bischoff fought the chemicals, but she also let her muscles relax and focused all her attention on her eyeballs. She found that if she held her awareness just right, she could control her irises. She dilated them. The abbots continued bustling around her, preparing vials and making notes. The equipment they used was unlike anything she had ever seen. The world had progressed in the years she'd been kept underground before the war, but not to this level of alien.

One of the men chuckled. "At least we know it can't kill her."

"No. She will be our greatest success."

"As long as we don't have a repeat of last time. She mustn't be allowed to bond again."

"That's what we're doing here." Deadpan.

The rest of the session was less painful than usual. They didn't seem to be doing anything to test her or find new limits to her abilities. After a hypnosis session that she now only pretended to follow, which took all her willpower and concentration to resist, Bischoff returned to her cell suspicious of what was really going on. For the first time, she felt nervous. Something big was coming.

It was way worse than the rabbit. If it had been another rabbit, Bischoff could have done it, just to keep the abbots believing that she was still under their control. The abbots talked about it as if she wasn't even in the room. Last time had been a test of strength. Now they needed to see if she would carry out an order. Any order.

Her father kneeled in the middle of the room, hands tied behind his back. He was not the strong, muscular man she remembered. One eye was bloodied shut, his lips swollen and split and bruises purpled his naked upper body. Bischoff ached to go to him.

"Kill him."

Bischoff stared at Papa as he raised his head, straining with the effort, to gaze at her. In his eyes she saw permission. When she gave a miniscule shake of her head, they changed. Wordlessly, he pleaded. She did not even think he did it consciously. The Papa she knew had already died in this place.

"Kill him." The order came again, stronger. They had given her nothing. She had only her supernaturally strong hands. She could squeeze his throat closed with her fingertips or crush his skull with a fist as easily as breaking eggshells. They waited, then watched her approach him. She knelt beside him and reached to stroke his matted hair.

"She won't do it. It hasn't worked." Two of the abbots pulled her off him and one of them slipped a needle into her neck. Caught off guard, she couldn't fight. She sank down into blackness. The last thing she saw before her eyes closed was another abbot slitting Papa's throat.

The burning was different this time. It lasted for days, indeterminate days, months, even. For once, Bischoff couldn't keep track of the time. There was no physical pain. It was something else, a tearing into pieces of the fabric of her being, shredding her soul. When she woke again, there was just a blackened hole where her heart had been. Bischoff lay on the cold gurney knowing she must leave, with or without a plan. She also knew she had to find the brother of a woman called Antonia Krenn, but she couldn't quite grasp why she'd ever decided to do that. Still. Abbot Johann finally came to see her, once it was reported that she was awake.

"You are special," he said, perched on a stool next to her bed. "You always were a gifted child, Ezzie."

"Don't call me that," Bischoff muttered, then wished she hadn't. She should be playing up the hazy state. Fortunately, Abbot Johann didn't seem to notice, or care. Perhaps he didn't fully understand what it meant for her to finally be able to say what she wanted.

"This is ground-breaking. You are the first of your kind. We don't know quite what you are, but you can't be killed by any means currently known to man. You are exceptionally strong and powerful, with enhanced senses, and your memory is remarkable. And now," he said, reaching to stroke her face, "you have been freed of the restraints of the heart. You can do what we ask without regard for what it is, or who it affects. You are our perfect weapon. This is just the beginning."

Bischoff took a moment to let this sink in. She thought about Mama and Papa. She knew, intellectually, that they had been important. They had raised her as a baby. But she couldn't recall any feelings for them. She remembered every man she'd killed on the battlefield and the guilt she'd felt afterward, how she hadn't wanted to fire the gun, but now the guilt was gone. She thought again of Krenn, and her baseless conviction to find Krenn's brother. She would do it, but she had no feeling about it. There was no love. Love receded into her mind as an abstract idea that perhaps had meaning for somebody else. What was still there was the anger, coiled in her like a viper. That, she realised, had never resided in her heart.

In the end it was easy. She told Johann that she was going to the toilet. He simply sat there while she walked out and shut the door behind her. Then she killed every single one of the abbots between her and the stairs. She washed the blood off her hands and arms in the Holy Water font, discarded her clothes on the floor of the baptistry and donned one of the spare abbot robes hanging in a closet in the office. 'Donovan' was stitched into a label on the inside of the collar. It was as good a name as any. She helped herself to the tithe chest on her way out, thinking she might be back, one day, to take care of Johann. Let him live in fear. Donovan, a new woman, emerged on the sunlit streets of Brno, 1919, hailed a taxi and set out to make someone atone for the Great War.

About the author

Kel E Fox ran an apothecary in a past life, was a stage technician in the theatre before she finally embraced writing in this life and hopes to be a wizard in the next. She is now part of what might be the world's only antisocial marketing team at Outfoxed Media and is working on her debut release The Lightning Event, the first of a YA-ish SF-esque trilogy about a girl who gets struck by lightning, develops superpowers, stumbles into a global conspiracy and meets an alien god all in the same day. Kel lives in Perth, Aus-

tralia with her life (and ballroom dancing) partner, two lazy cats and a wilful young Alaskan Malamute named after Nighteyes. As it happens, The Inheritance Experiment is a sort of prequel to The Lightning Event, so if you enjoy your read here, you just might like the trilogy too! The Lightning Event is due for release in 2019, all going well. You can keep up to date on Kel's news and nonsense by subscribing to her newsletter (which she hasn't written yet) at outfoxedmedia.com.au/novels or find her on Facebook and Twitter @kelelizabethfox.

Bus Trip

Stephen Herczeg

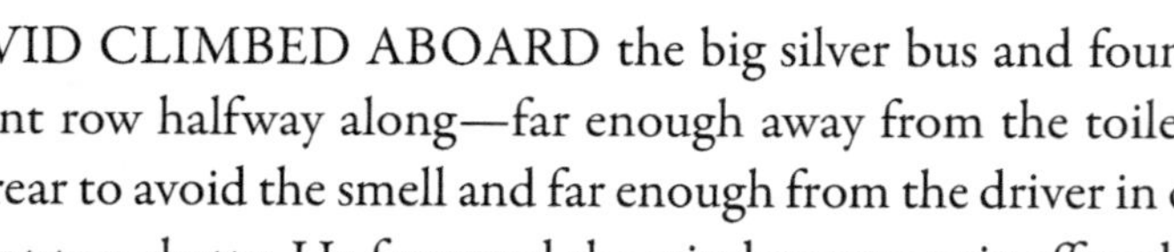

DAVID CLIMBED ABOARD the big silver bus and found a vacant row halfway along—far enough away from the toilet at the rear to avoid the smell and far enough from the driver in case he got too chatty. He favoured the window seat as it offered the extra stimulation of viewing the countryside passing by, though most of the trip would be through the desolate wastelands of the Hay Plains.

He plonked down and pulled out his book for the journey. Reading the title *Fourier series of the Periodic Bernoulli and Euler Functions* he sighed. A sixteen-hour bus trip and the dynamic world of applied mathematics to keep him company.

Movement in the aisle dragged his attention away from the riveting read, and he looked up into a pair of sparkling blue eyes framed by long blonde hair.

"David, isn't it?" the owner of the eyes asked.

David immediately recognised the girl as Hannah, a fellow student from his chemistry class. Her eyes passed over his book and a smile played on her lips.

"Nice book. Applied Maths three next year, right?" she asked.

David nodded.

"Yep. With Professor Chan. Meant to be tough so I thought I'd read up before term starts. Also thought it would put me to sleep pretty damn quick," he said.

Hannah laughed. She indicated the seat next to David. "Is this taken?"

"Not at all," he said, "hang on." He rose and shuffled out from the window seat. "You can have the window, I think my book will provide enough stimulation for my tired mind."

"Thanks," she said, edging into the window seat.

As they conversed, they realised they had lived close to each other for the best part of their lives. The only reason they had never met was because their parents' houses were on opposite sides of the boundary, forcing them to attend different schools.

Because of that, Hannah's parents had found the money to send her to an exclusive private girls' school rather than attend the state school. Her grades had been so good that she'd qualified for a scholarship and ended up at the Australian National University, along with David.

They talked for what seemed like half an hour, but when they pulled into the Gundagai roadhouse they both realised it had been closer to two hours. Hannah smiled as the buildings near the *Dog on the Tucker Box* came into sight.

"I need to stretch my legs," she said.

They both moved outside and grabbed what passed as a coffee in the roadhouse. Between gulps of the steaming hot liquid, they continued their conversation. Taking a chance, David suggested they share a cab when they reached the bus station in Adelaide. Hannah agreed with a wistful smile on her lips and playfully moved a lock of her long blonde hair away from her face and behind her ear.

She excused herself and moved off to the bathrooms, glancing back towards David before moving into the building.

David's chest only managed to hold onto his swiftly beating heart through sheer willpower. There was something there—with Hannah. It was only a spark, but it could be the start of something huge in his life.

Back on the bus, their conversation eventually lulled into silence. David's attention turned to his textbook, while Hannah made a pillow out of her jumper and curled up for a nap. The paragraphs of dense text and complicated formulae before David's eyes blurred into the scribblings of a three-year-old. All he could see, in his mind's eye, was that smile, those eyes and that lock of hair.

Finally, the textbook took its toll and his eyelids drooped and closed sending him into dreamland where images of Hannah swirled amongst the lines of mathematical equations, equations that formed a timeline of possibilities that ended with him and Hannah in a dreamland paradise for the rest of their lives.

DAVID AWOKE WITH A start and checked his watch. Four hours had passed since the bus left Gundagai. He looked through the window.

Outside wide-open plains covered in brown grass stretched off to the horizon that consisted of mile after mile of rolling brown hills. A river wound its way through the hills, its banks home to small copses of green tipped eucalypts. It was stark, but in a beautiful way.

Yep, we could be anywhere.

His eyes dropped to Hannah. She was asleep as well. Her head lolled against the window, jiggling with the movement of the bus. He peered around to check if anyone was watching, then turned his attention back to her. He stared and admired the lines of her face, her high cheekbones, her long lashes and flowing flaxen hair.

She's so beautiful. She'd never go for a dope like me. But there was something there. She smiled. And she wants to share a cab.

He checked the rest of the bus again. Everybody else seemed to be asleep as well. Even to someone who had taken this trip so many times it seemed odd, usually there was some movement; the tinny sound of music coming from a pair of headphones, or the hum of idle chatter. Something, but the only sounds he heard were the road noise rising through the floor and the only movement was the scenery flashing by outside.

He turned his gaze back to Hannah. His eyes traced every curve and line on her face. He glanced down further for a moment, but his timidity with women forced them back to her face. That's when he noticed it.

He craned forward for a better look.

Hannah had a small white blemish beneath her left eye. David moved in closer and examined the discolouration. He found it mildly exciting that someone so flawless had an imperfection.

Suddenly, the small white patch moved.

David flinched, the heavy textbook slipped off his lap and thumped to the floor.

"Bugger," he said out loud.

He looked down and tried to reach for the book. His out-stretched fingers brushed the edge and accidentally pushed it further away. He glanced across at Hannah to see if he'd woken her.

His mouth dropped open and his eyes grew wide in shock as he leaned in for a closer look.

The skin beneath Hannah's eye pulsated as if alive with a will of its own.

"Hannah?" David said and reached out for her shoulder.

Suddenly, the skin burst open and a small white creature with a black head wriggled out of the hole. David reeled back in abject horror. His foot shot out and kicked the book further down towards the front of the bus.

He stared back at the thing on Hannah's face.

A maggot.

David gagged at the sight. His hand went to his mouth to quell an ejection of vomit. He watched, fascinated, as the maggot wiggled across Hannah's cheek and slipped off into her hair.

He reached out with his other hand and gave the sleeping girl a slight nudge.

"Hannah?" he asked again. She stayed still—the maggot was the only movement.

David's fear grew.

She's dead.

He reached out, grabbed her shoulder and shook. He wanted to wake her up, to make sure she was still alive. She stayed still, scaring him even more. In his panic, he shook harder.

Suddenly, her skin ripped open from cheek to neck. Blood and maggots poured from the wound and spilled across her chest.

David jumped out of his seat and gaped. Revulsion stirred his stomach and terror consumed his mind. The woman that mere hours ago was so full of life and beauty, now sat split open amidst a teeming mass of maggots.

"Hannah?" he cried. His stomach convulsed and let fly. He filled his now vacant seat with his lunch, breakfast and last night's dinner. The vile smelling liquid splashing across the seething mass that was now Hannah. He coughed, spitting the final dregs into his seat and stood up.

Hannah's chest and lap were now a sea of writhing white maggots bathed in Hannah's red life-blood. As he watched, her body deflated and began to slip off the seat.

In a panic, he turned and grabbed the arm of the reclining man next to him. He shook the man to try to wake him.

"Sir, please help, sir," he shouted staring back as Hannah's body collapsed in on itself.

The man continued to doze.

David shook harder. His plea was met with a sharp crack as the man's arm tore away from his shoulder. Blood sprayed from the wound, bathing David's pants in a fine red shower. David screamed and dropped the arm. It flopped to the floor at his feet.

He looked at the man's face. The skin started peeling away in ragged clumps of red, revealing the meat and bone beneath. More maggots pushed out of the muscles and crawled across the open flesh.

David simply stared open-mouthed for a moment. He gagged in revulsion, but there was nothing left to bring up.

He backed away down the aisle. All thoughts of his book and of Hannah banished from his mind. He needed safety. He needed to retreat from the carnal nightmare before him. He glanced at the passengers on either side. And screamed again.

All four people were disintegrating into pools of accelerated decay. Their facial skin sloughing off and falling into their laps amidst a waterfall of blood and mucus as he stepped past.

David turned and raced towards the driver. He blinkered his vision to avoid glancing at the devastated bodies of the other passengers on either side, but glimpses of putrescence seeped into his peripheral vision. He gulped, put his head down and proceeded to the front.

David hunkered down beside the driver's seat. Behind the Perspex screen, the driver ignored him and continued to stare at the road ahead. David tapped on the plastic and tried to sound calm, so he could be understood.

"Hey, Sir," David said, "there's people back there. Dead people. You need to do something."

The driver's face remained fixed, staring straight ahead. David rapped harder and raised his voice.

"Sir, they are dead and ..." he stifled a cry of hysteria, "rotting, Sir."

The driver continued to ignore him. David's terror gave way to anger. He made a fist and pounded on the window.

"Hey," he shouted and finally got a reaction. The driver's head slowly turned towards him. David fell backwards in horror. The driver's face was missing, replaced by white bone and empty eye sockets. Small flaps of red-tinged skin and muscle hung from the bone. Trails of red dribbled down the man's remaining face. David caught a glimpse of the facial meat resting in the driver's lap and threatening to drop under the bus's pedals.

"Oh my God," David gulped.

He got to his feet, turned and grabbed the entrance door handle.

"Let me out."

He shook the handle with all his might. Nothing. He screamed and hit the door, in anger, with the palm of his hand.

He turned around. The driver was still looking at him, his rictus grin chilled David to the bone. Slowly, the driver's head turned back to face the road. David followed his stare. The open countryside rolled towards them in endless waves of brown dirt and grass.

At least outside it's still normal.

David looked up the aisle towards the rear window.

I gotta get out.

He took off, stumbling towards the back of the bus. He kept his eyes directed at the rear, ignoring the dead bodies on either side. He tripped on something and fell forward. His hand landed on the dismembered arm eliciting a slight scream from his ravaged throat. He pushed the arm aside and looked back at his feet.

His stupid textbook lay several feet away, where it had come to rest after he'd tripped on it.

Damn maths.

He got to his feet and saw movement towards the back of the bus. A man was moving towards the toilet.

Someone else. Someone like me.

"Hey, Sir," shouted David. He lurched towards the man, almost losing his feet as the bus rocked and rolled. David reached a hand out towards the man's shoulder. The bus bucked and threw him off balance. His hand landed in the middle of the man's back pitching them both forwards.

A loud crack reverberated over the road noise. The man's head bent backwards and flopped against his back. A pair of accusing eyes stared into David's for a moment before the last pieces of gristle snapped and the head dropped to the floor and rolled towards him. He jumped back in terror. The eyes remained fixed on his with an unblinking stare for a moment, then the skin let go and peeled away revealing more bone and meat. The man's body teetered and then fell forward with a resounding thump.

Tears streamed down David's face as his confused brain tried to process everything. He looked up from the decapitated man and focused on the rear window. The emergency exit.

He made his way past the remaining seats, mercifully empty with no further atrocities to greet him.

He looked at the window. The handles to pull the window out were on the exterior to aid emergency workers. A small note said: In case of emergency kick glass out.

David sidled up, kicked with all his might and bounced backwards. The window stubbornly stayed fixed in place. He steadied himself and managed to land a stronger kick. The window bucked and shifted a little. He smiled and stepped back a few paces. He turned, dropped his shoulder and ran forward as fast as he could. As luck would have it, the bus rocked at the same moment adding momentum to David's run.

He hit the window with such force that both he and it exploded from the bus.

The wind burst from his lungs as he hit the road. A crack in his shoulder was met with a flash of pain that streaked through his mind. He rolled several times before coming to a stop and gingerly got to his knees. The bus continued down the road, throwing up a plume of dust as if he'd never been aboard.

David peered around at the barren landscape. Another streak of pain hit, he winced in agony and put a hand to his injured shoulder. He tried to work out where he was and figured he was somewhere between Narrandera and Hay. His shoulders slumped at the prospect of up to a hundred kilometres of road standing between him and the nearest town.

He turned and began walking towards the setting sun.

The sound of a car made him turn and gingerly hold out a thumb. An older model Falcon crested a nearby rise and approached him. He shook his thumb and looked hopefully at the driver. They made brief eye contact and the car pulled over. David staggered to the car and got into the rear seat.

An elderly couple looked over the front seats at him with bright smiles on their faces.

"Gidday, I'm Tony and this is my wife Jan," said the driver. His face turned to a look of concern. "Haven't seen any cars for miles, so what the hell are you doing out here on your own, young feller?"

David coughed and replied, "I fell out of a bus."

The couple laughed.

"Good one," said Tony. He turned around and said, over his shoulder, "well buckle up, we're stopping in Hay in about an hour. Get comfortable. Hope you like fifties music cause that's all we have."

He pulled out onto the highway and started to drive. A couple of sharp guitar chords rang out of the speakers behind David's head and Elvis Presley's voice sang the first lines of *Jailhouse Rock*.

Not the most relaxing music, but David ignored it as he sat back, stared out the window at the landscape zooming by and tried to take it all in. To his fevered mind the day was too insane to be real. Maybe it wasn't. Maybe it was all just a dream. Maybe he was still dreaming. Maybe he had fallen out of the bus. Maybe Hannah was okay. Maybe there was hope that he could find her again.

He sighed deeply and focused on the two people in the front. Jan's head was just a ball of dark hair, but Tony was bald, and the shining skin showed through the hole in the headrest.

David noticed a small patch of white skin on the back of Tony's head. His eyes grew wide. He leaned forward and studied the back of the driver's head.

He'd seen a white spot like it not long ago.

Suddenly, it moved.

David screamed.

About the author

Stephen is an IT Geek, writer, actor and film maker based in Canberra Australia. He has been writing for over twenty years and has completed a couple of dodgy novels, sixteen feature length screenplays and numerous short stories and scripts.

Stephen was very successful in 2017's International Horror Hotel screenplay competition, with his scripts TITAN winning the Sci-Fi category and Dark are the Woods placing second in the horror category.

His work has featured in Sproutlings – A compendium of little fictions from Hunter Anthologies, the Hells Bells Christmas horror anthology published by the Australasian Horror Writers Association and the Below the Stairs, Trickster's Treats #1 and #2, Shades of Santa, Behind the Mask and Beyond the Infinite anthologies from OzHorror.Con, The Body Horror Book, Anemone Enemy and Petrified Punks from Oscillate Wildly Press and has had Sherlock Holmes stories published in Sherlock Holmes in the realms of H.G. Wells, Sherlock Holmes: Adventures beyond the Canon and The MX Book of New Sherlock Holmes stories: Part XI from Belanger Books.

Stephen is elated to have his story Bus Trip featured in the Australian Speculative Fiction Anthology – Beginnings.

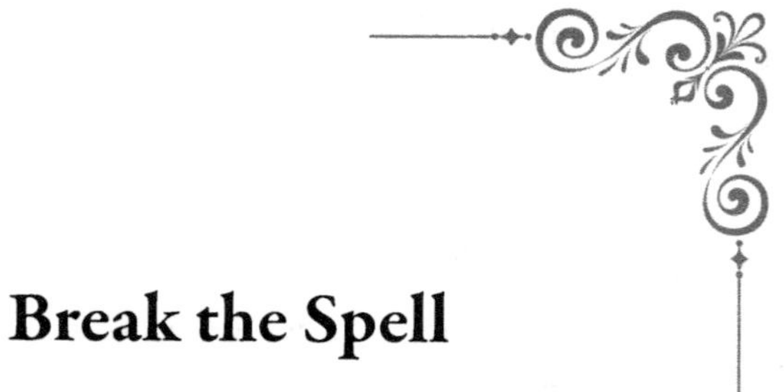

Break the Spell

Belinda Brady

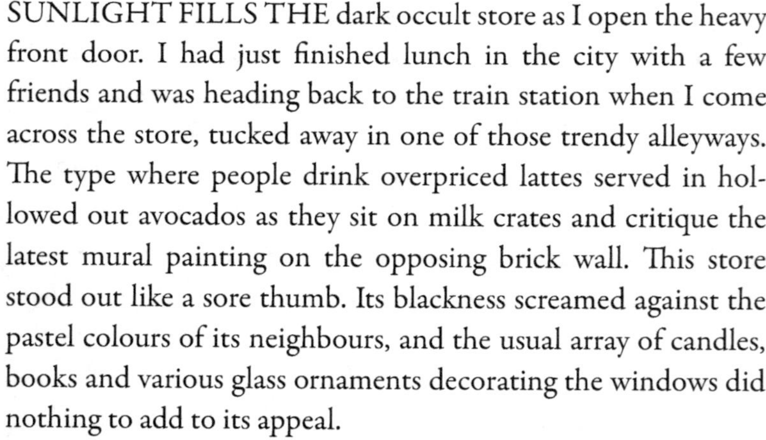

SUNLIGHT FILLS THE dark occult store as I open the heavy front door. I had just finished lunch in the city with a few friends and was heading back to the train station when I come across the store, tucked away in one of those trendy alleyways. The type where people drink overpriced lattes served in hollowed out avocados as they sit on milk crates and critique the latest mural painting on the opposing brick wall. This store stood out like a sore thumb. Its blackness screamed against the pastel colours of its neighbours, and the usual array of candles, books and various glass ornaments decorating the windows did nothing to add to its appeal.

These stores are a dime a dozen and can be found in any town on the map, but this one was different. Normally, I'd cross the street to avoid a place like this, but for some reason I just *had* to go inside. Worse case, I buy a few crystals, maybe even a spell and then I'll have a story to tell the girls at our next catch up. My friends were always telling funny, 'this happened to me stories;' maybe I'd finally have one to tell? Maybe I'd finally be the funny one they are laughing with, instead of being boring old me, sitting there with my usual, 'nothing new with me' stories.

Taking a deep breath, I adjust my jacket and hold my head up high as I leave the brightness of the street and enter the store. I'm surprised by how small, but brimming with goods, the place is. Every shelf, every corner, every table has *something* on it—books, crystals, tarot cards, and knickknacks the likes of which I had never seen—this store had it all. I make my way to the back of the store, coming across a bookshelf simply titled '*Spells*', and after scanning the titles on offer, my finger rests on a book called '*Classic Love Spells*'. Leafing through it, I stop at a spell titled '*Love Me Back*' and am surprised to see it only requires minimal items, many of which can be found in any kitchen—even my pathetically understocked kitchen. I couldn't tell you the last time I had a proper date, and when I did, he spent the whole time organising hook ups on his phone, offering me the odd murmur of conversation as he did so. I didn't bother trying again after that. But, I have been feeling lonely lately, and watching my girlfriends flash their engagement rings and hand out wedding invites always gives me a pang of fear. What if there is no one out there for me and I am doomed to die alone? That fear hits me again as I stare at the spell, and before I can stop myself, I grab the book.

"Besides, what's the worst thing that can happen? I end up happily ever after?" I mutter to myself as I walk over to the unenthusiastic sales clerk, who only manages to grumble, "Hey," at me—or possibly his computer screen—throughout our entire transaction.

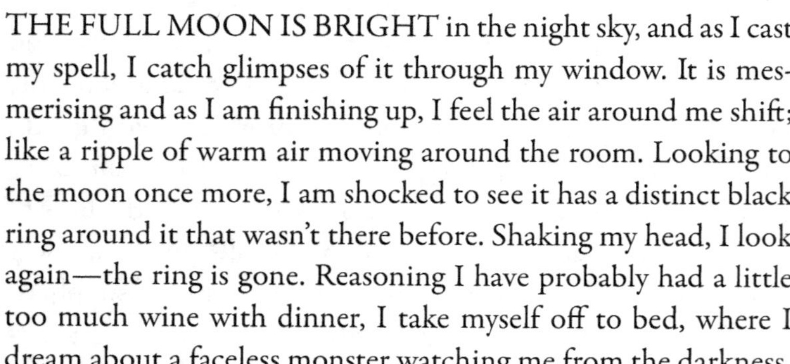

THE FULL MOON IS BRIGHT in the night sky, and as I cast my spell, I catch glimpses of it through my window. It is mesmerising and as I am finishing up, I feel the air around me shift; like a ripple of warm air moving around the room. Looking to the moon once more, I am shocked to see it has a distinct black ring around it that wasn't there before. Shaking my head, I look again—the ring is gone. Reasoning I have probably had a little too much wine with dinner, I take myself off to bed, where I dream about a faceless monster watching me from the darkness.

IT'S SATURDAY MORNING and I'm having coffee in my usual café when I see him, tucked away in the corner reading the paper. He's been blessed with light brown hair peppered with a few greys that just adds to his looks and friendly brown eyes that crinkle when he smiles. He is gorgeous. He drinks coffee. He is breathing. He is *perfect*. I position myself at a table near this mystery man, unsure of my next move. Two coffees and no contact later, I'm cursing myself for not being brave enough to approach him, when I'm aware of someone standing by my table. Looking up, my heart flips—it's him.

"Hi." He smiles, flashing impossibly white teeth and extending a hand. "I just thought I'd come over and introduce myself. I'm Tate, nice to meet you."

I return the smile and take his hand, reminding myself to keep my cool. "Hi, I'm Melody. It's nice to meet you too."

His touch is warm and I instantly feel at ease, as though I have known him my whole life. We fall into easy conversation and talk all afternoon where, after getting kicked out of the café as it was closing, we finish up at a local bar over a few drinks. Parting, we exchange numbers and make plans to meet up for Sunday breakfast. I've never met anyone I click with so quickly, and when he texts me five minutes after we've said our goodbyes, stating he misses me already, I practically float home—images of children, dogs and white picket fences dancing around my head.

This is it! This is really it!

BREAKFAST QUICKLY TURNED into another date, and then another. We are soon inseparable. Tate tells me he loves me after one week. I have been waiting so long to hear those words, but something just doesn't sit right. Tate seems too keen, too soon. There are so many red flags; he calls and texts me constantly—sometimes up to fifty times a day—just to see what I am doing, what I am wearing, and who I am with. He sends bunches of flowers to my workplace every day—huge declarations of love for all to see, which I accept with a fake smile plastered on my face, while fear churns away silently in my stomach. This relationship is the one I have dreamed about my entire life, the one I have been waiting for, but it just feels wrong, *so* wrong. It keeps me in a constant state of anxiety, making sleep near impossible and when I finally do fall asleep, my dreams are haunted by a shadowy beast, one I can't see, but can hear, as he relentlessly screams my name from the darkness.

The final straw comes when I casually mention one day that I often have lunch with a male workmate. The look on Tate's face as his nostrils flare and his whole body tenses terrifies me. I *have* to get out. This is a whole new level of love—a scary love—and I want no part of it. But I have to be smart. I am worried about how Tate will react when I break it off. Until I have a solution, I keep up the charade of the happy girlfriend, whilst Tate's obsessive love grows in leaps and bounds. He is making plans to give notice on his lease and move in, that way "there'd be no little secrets and we'd be together all the time." The only thing that matters to me is how to end this and walk away unscathed, and as I lie in bed one night going over possible scenarios for the millionth time, the solution hits me out of the blue.

"The spell!" I shriek, sitting upright with a bolt. "The spell! I need to reverse the spell!"

Suddenly, it all makes perfect sense, and thanks to a family emergency that has taken Tate out of town, I have some precious time to myself to put this solution into practice. A spell had brought this nightmare into my life, and a spell was going to take him out of it.

I'M WAITING AT THE front door of the occult store, the place where all my troubles started, when it finally opens. The same sales clerk who sold me the book opens the heavy front door, jumping back in surprise when he sees me.

"Oh hey!" he exclaims. "I wasn't expecting anyone to be here, but welcome. Come on in." He smiles as he holds the door open for me. I don't return the smile. I'm on a mission. I

burst into the store, and storm into the *'Spells'* section, frantically searching for my spell breaker. After what seems like an eternity of looking through books and spell bags, my stomach sinks
as it appears I'm not going to find my saviour. With my anxiety
rising to eruption levels, I look to the sales clerk, who is trying
his best to ignore me, and rush over to him.

"Excuse me, Ben," I breathe, reading his nametag. "I need
some help finding ... I need some help—," my voice trails off. I
feel like such a fool for even asking, but then my phone beeps
with a text. It's from Tate;

*'Hey! I've tried calling you at work to check in and they said
you've called in sick? Where are you??? What are you doing???
Who are you with??? I'm really not happy about this Melody. Call
me immediately! I'll be home first thing in the morning, but before
then I want some answers.'*

In spite of my best efforts to keep it together, I burst into
tears. Ben awkwardly offers me some tissues, which I gratefully
accept.

"Listen, Ben. I cast a love spell a few weeks back. A spell that
was in a book I bought from this store, but I need to break the
spell. It has turned bad and I need it gone. Please tell me I can
break this spell. Can you help me?" I splutter as a wipe away my
tears.

Ben takes a sip of his coffee as he studies me.

"What book was it?"

I reach into my handbag and slam the offending book on
the counter. "This! This one! The spell I cast is the *'Love Me
Back'* spell."

Studying the book he muses, "Ah, yes this one. We've had a few complaints about this book. Seems the spells work a little … ah, a little *too* well. You could almost say it's a hex in disguise. I thought we had gotten rid of them all … guess not."

I look at him stunned—I'm not the only one?

"Lucky for you, I have just the thing you need," he continues as he hands over a black, satin bag. "This contains all you need to break the spell. But, as is the story with most spells, this needs to be performed on the night of a full moon, which just so happens to be tonight. Great timing huh?"

I'm so relieved I could almost kiss him, but instead I throw my money on the counter and thank him profusely as I rush out of the store, heading home to await the night's full moon.

THE FULL MOON LIGHTS up the night, as I cast the reversal spell with a growing sense of deja vu. . Once I'm finished, just like before, the air around me has a certain thickness to it, that same ripple but stronger. Looking at the moon, I see it has two black rings around it, one darker than the other. It's almost ominous, familiar even. Putting my head down, I take a few deep breaths, trying to figure out where I had seen them before, when the realisation makes me snap my head back up. These rings, and the ones I had seen when I cast that first spell, are all part of the spell, part of the magic, though I don't remember the second, darker ring being there that first time. And just like before, I see the rings are now gone. Satisfied the spell has been successfully cast, I pack up and head off to bed for some much needed rest. I've put all I had into this spell and I am exhausted. I fall into a fitful sleep, where the hidden monster in my dream is close, so close I can feel it's breath on my neck, but I still can't see it.

I AWAKE TO A BEAUTIFUL Saturday morning to find a long text message from Tate. After I texted him the night before stating I was simply too sick to talk to him, I'm expecting a nasty reply but as I read it, a huge smile spreads across my face. Tate had broken up with me. He realised he wasn't ready to commit and needed to rediscover himself—in India. I stare at the message, not quite believing the words, but there they are, staring back at me from my phone. He is leaving me and is flying out the next day. The spell has been broken! He is gone! I am so damn happy. I decide a mini celebration is in order—a day of food, chocolate, and shopping, all washed down with a few glasses of wine. My soul desperately needs to be spoilt. Deciding to dress for the occasion, I'm putting on my favourite dress, when I realise I feel a little odd, almost like I have been drugged. I stand there until it passes, it must be stress. And who wouldn't be stressed after going through this horrible experience? Brushing off any concern, I get dressed, grab my purse and practically skip to the front door.

Today is going to be such a special day.

THE SALES CLERK WATCHES the front door intently. He knows she'll be coming into the store soon and, right on cue, there she is. She looks stunning in that dress. She opens the door and walks straight toward him, a look of certainty on her face.

"Excuse me, Ben? This may seem a little forward, but, would you like to join me for a coffee when you have a break?" she says, smiling that gorgeous smile of hers.

"Sure, I would love to. I get off in five minutes, so if you just wait, I'll be right with you."

She smiles as she turns away from him, busying herself with some books on display.

He too smiles, but for a different reason. Silently congratulating himself, Ben pats the last copy of 'Classic Love Spells' that is hidden out of sight under the counter. The 'Love Me Back' spell is bookmarked. More than one spell was cast last night, and the power of this spell increased tenfold since he'd had a tissue she left on the counter. The magic was always stronger when an item that either belonged to, or had been touched by, the one you were casting the spell on was used, permanently binding you to them. Regardless of your intentions.

Which is just what Ben wanted.

Ben had loved Melody the moment he saw her. He knew she was different. She would listen, she would obey, and she wouldn't try to leave. This was a new beginning. And as he put on his coat to accompany Melody to coffee, imagining the life he was about to create, and ultimately control, with the girl of his dreams, Ben knew this was one spell that was not going to be broken.

About the author

Belinda is passionate about stories and after years of procrastinating, has finally turned her hand to writing them, with a prefer-

ence for supernatural and thriller themes; her love of both often competing for her attention. She has had several stories published in print, online and in anthologies, in a variety of publications. Belinda lives in Australia with her family, and has been known to enjoy the company of cats over people.

Portals

A. A. Warne

WIDE EYED AND STARING at the ceiling, Jon hadn't slept in weeks. He had spent most of the night chewing down his nails until he reached the nail bed, then changed fingers and began again. He couldn't remember the last time he had stomached a proper meal. Food, sleep, and anything mundane were the last things on his mind.

Frustrated, he ran his hands through his hair, pushing back the brown tufts as he sat up. He humphed out heavy, laboured breaths, in and out, and wished he was some place other than here.

Looking over to the far side of the room, where his twin sisters slept in each other's arms, chasing their own world of dreams. Seeing them, he regretted his wish. He came back for a reason: to protect his family.

Getting to his feet quietly, Jon looked down at them. Their brown locks wrapped around their soft innocent faces and they didn't even twitch with him pacing the room. His hand went straight back to his mouth. He fought the nervous urge only to find himself biting down again.

In the room beside his, he could hear long drawn out breaths of his sleeping parents, and on the other side of the hall, his grandmother had just clicked out her light. How could they sleep peacefully every night when he suffered? He paced—one foot in front of the other—until he reached the wall, turned, then marched back the other way.

Had his disappearance not bothered them? Did they even care if he stayed or snuck out again during high moon, not returning for another twelve nights?

When he had returned home, giving no explanation for leaving without any notice whatsoever, is that when his family began sleeping again?

Jon couldn't blame them. It was his fault and he knew that. And as each day came and went, ticking by like nothing ever happened, the heavy torment that sat on his chest, weighed him down even more.

Questioning just how many more days he could live like this, he looked down at himself and wondered what happened. The meat on his bones had disappeared. The mirror above the washbasin showed him looking more dead than alive. Running his fingers through his hair, chunks fell out. He was thinning rapidly. For a man of only nineteen heat seasons, he felt aged.

He stopped pacing. He stopped thinking. He just stopped.

Tilting his head back and closing his eyes, Jon held his hands out to the side, and whispered to the Gods.

They didn't answer.

Instead, an idea popped into his mind. Like a tiny seed sprouting inside his head, Jon latched onto it and shaped it into a decision. In the morning, first thing, he would speak to Yalda and tell her exactly what happened to her son, even if it will get Jon killed.

His lungs expanded. The fresh air filled his nostrils, entered his body and he instantly felt lighter, even a smile spread across his face.

He turned towards his bed. Sleep welcomed him into its embrace and he lunged for it desperately.

"Jon." A voice spoke.

Jon cracked one eye open.

"Jon, wake up now!"

Jon recognised his father's panicked voice and sprung up out of bed ready to fight. He latched onto his father's arms, trying to steady his nerves. "What's that noise?"

There was a sound in the distance, and it was unlike anything he'd ever heard. A deep vibration, low and consistent, hummed across the entire city. Then its pitch became higher and the sound became louder, somewhere between a kettle screeching under pressure and a goat screaming before a slaughter. Without warning it lowered again, into a deep rumble that could be felt right through to his very core.

The girls cried out from their beds. Their mother rushed to them, clinging onto them for comfort. She looked to her husband and son. The sheer panic in her eyes scared Jon more than the distant noise.

"Portals." His grandmother stood in the doorway. "They've come."

Still holding onto his father, Jon felt him shake.

"Get what you want girls," his father yelled at them. "And hurry!"

The girls, most likely too frightened to move, latched onto their mother and reached for their soft, cuddly bed toys.

"Jon," his father looked to him. "My only son."

"Yes, father."

"I never wanted this day to come." He pulled Jon into a warm embrace. "But I want you to promise me something."

"Of course, father." Jon said, pulling back to look into his father's eyes. "Anything."

"You are my son, and I'm so proud of the man you have turned out to be. Take pride in what you do and live your life. Remember us with love."

"Always," Jon whispered.

"But son," his father's voice now firm. "Don't dwell on what cannot be changed."

Jon dropped his head, avoiding his father's eyes. His father, a smart and gentle man, knew Jon was in some sort of trouble but never pressed the matter. Even after Jon's disappearance, his father cried when he returned and welcomed him with open arms. The guilt sat like a hard rock in the pit of his stomach, growing larger, stronger, fiercer by the moment. Painfully aware that he didn't turn out to be the honourable son his father deserved, Jon couldn't lift his head; instead, slightly bobbed his head up and down to agree.

"Stand children," Grandmother spoke, and they all turned to listen. "We mustn't linger. You know the rules. All who stay will suffer the penalty of death."

The girls bellowed out, crying into their mother's chest.

"Hush, Ma Ma," his mother scolded. "We know."

"Then get up, we need to go," Grandmother ordered and without a fight, the family stood and reluctantly went through the front door.

The moon—high above in the sky—lit a soft path in the midnight darkness. Clustered together, the neighbouring families spilled out onto the streets. Marching side by side in the same direction, leaving behind the only thing they'd ever known.

The vibration, loud and low, shook through each of their bodies.

Jon walked between his father and grandmother, his mother not far ahead of them had a twin on each arm. One looked up to their mother, and Jon could see the tears on her cheek.

"What's going to happen?" whispered his sister.

Their mother stopped in the middle of the road, bending down to his sisters' level.

"Keep walking Meena," Jon's father scolded, helping her to her feet and continued the shuffle along. She dragged the girls beside her, clutching them tighter than before.

"I don't know sweethearts," she said as her voice rattled. "As the Law of the Universe states, when the portals arrive, everyone must enter or thou shall be sentenced to death. So we will do just that. Go through the portal, my loves, and hopefully I'll see you on the other side." She pressed her lips to their foreheads, as tears soaked her already wet cheeks.

A lump in Jon's throat formed as he could see her pain, tears of his own threatening to fall. At that moment, as if sensing his own fear, his mother turned to him and winked. He smiled back at her, comforted by her lie.

The crowd walked silently, hanging on dearly to their loved ones. Sobs broke the silence while everyone marched towards the portal. The feeling of dread was strong, with no other choice but to keep going.

Jon searched the faces of his neighbours. A voice in the back of his mind reminded him that he may never see a single one of them again. The luck of staying with a loved one, let alone a neighbour, was slim to none.

Several groups away, he locked eyes with Lada. She had her hair twisted up around her head and beside her, wrapped around her arm, was her elderly father. Struggling to walk with his crooked leg, he limped his way down the street, falling into line with everyone else.

Jon had never told Lada how much she meant to him. Her father forbade it. Seeing how much she cared for the old man, Jon decided it was best to wait out the old man's life before sweeping her off her feet and giving her the life she deserved.

"I need to say goodbye to Lada." Jon turned to his father, squeezed his hand and then pushed his way through the crowd to stand before her.

"Not you again," the old crow barked.

"Jon?" Her sweet voice lifted his heart as she said his name.

"I told you before boy…"

"What do you mean Papa?" she scolded her father. The old man flashed his guilty eyes, bowing down under her glare.

She stopped walking and let go of her father.

Jon didn't want to waste time on the man, he only had time for Lada.

"I'm sorry Lada. I know I never told you how I felt, that we never had a chance to create a life together. But I'll never forget you." He leant in, hesitant to watch for a sign she wanted him to stop. She squashed all of his concerns when she pulled him close. Wrapping his arms tightly around her waist, he pressed his lips to hers.

She stepped back and whispered. "You will forever remain in my heart."

Jon couldn't open his eyes and look at her again. If he did, he wouldn't have the strength to face the portal knowing it'd be the last time he'd see her. He'd end up fighting to keep her here and that would get them both killed. So he kept his head down as he whispered goodbye. He turned his back, leaving her with her father, and rushed back to his own family—not daring to look back.

His father put an arm around his shoulder while his grandmother reached out to take his hand.

"In all my years," she said. "I'd never thought I'd see this day come to pass." She pressed a cloth to her eyes, sweeping away the tears.

"We've had a good life," his father mused. "And I wish you all the best in your life to come."

"If I could sacrifice my life to keep you all together," Grandmother cried. "Then consider me dead."

"We'll be fine," Jon said. "You've raised us well." His guilt rose again, and wished he at least told his father. He was a man full of answers, but Jon just couldn't ask the questions. As they continued their march towards the other side of town, more people joined the growing crowd.

His father wrapped his arm around Jon's shoulders and squeezed. Jon wanted to give the love back, knowing it was his only chance. But the guilt of running away, of causing the pain in his father's heart, would never be mended.

Jon scanned the crowd again. Watching other people's pain was easier than dealing with his own. From the corner of his eye, he saw someone looking back. It was the one person he'd been avoiding for weeks. The person who caused him to run in the first place. Vít.

Jon knew a secret. One that got Leoš killed.

Vít stood at the furthest edge of the crowd and stared directly at Jon. His face cold as the day he killed Leoš.

Jon's stomach dropped.

Vít narrowed his eyes and focused on Jon.

The fear of Vít catching up with him was what stopped Jon from returning home. But then Jon realised Vít would hurt his family to draw him out of hiding. So he returned. But his secret, the guilt of keeping that secret hurt in more ways that he realised. He couldn't eat, hadn't been to the toilet, felt his insides as a mix-match mess and no longer slept. He was a living ghost.

Jon looked away from those demanding eyes, feeling them on his face, he gazed towards the portal and sent his wishes out to the universe.

"Please don't send me anywhere with Vít or I'm as good as dead." He whispered under his breath.

Then he remembered what he'd planned on doing that morning. Yalda needed to know the truth about her son. Jon found Yalda's face in the crowd further up the busy road, on the other side of the crowd to where Vít was standing. He etched a plan in his mind, but needed to get to her quickly. She was close to the portal and it wouldn't be long before she went through.

"Father," Jon turned to him. "I need to right the wrongs I have done. I need ..."

"Do whatever it is you must and remember, if I don't ever see you again, always remember that no matter what, I love you."

His mother turned around and cried out. "No ..."

Jon leaned in and kissed his mother on the forehead, hugged his father tightly, and then scuffed up the girls' hairs, which they hated. He leaned in and whispered to his grandmother. "Kick arse wherever you are."

She laughed and he turned away, knowing he'd never see them again.

Jon ducked his head down below the crowd so that Vít couldn't see him. Pushing his way through the crowd, Jon headed towards Yalda.

Jon rattled his brain on whether it was worth telling her or not. They were about to go through the portal and be redistributed throughout the universe. Was it worth the risk when he would start his life over afresh?

He stopped and popped his head up to see if he was still heading the right way. When he did, he realised that he had given Vít the chance to seen him. Turning to confirm his fears, Jon saw that Vít was halfway towards him already.

Panicked, Jon pushed his way through the crowd. Forcing people out of the way, he screamed out to Yalda—he was no longer uncertain about what he must tell her. She stopped walking and turned. The crowd around her kept moving, not daring to take the risk.

"Yalda!"

"Jon!" She grabbed hold of him. The shock in her eyes rattled Jon. They latched onto one another and Jon pulled Yalda towards the portal.

"We have to hurry," Jon said. "There's not much time."

"Shouldn't we slow down then."

Jon looked over his shoulder and saw Vít push people violently out of the way. "No!"

Noticing that Yalda wasn't as fast as him, Jon linked arms and helped her keep pace.

"Yalda, I need to tell you the truth." He said.

"Why? What's going on?" She looked to Vít then back to Jon. "Do you know something about my Leoš?"

"Yes," Jon said, swallowing the lump in his throat. The moment had arrived—the moment of truth. He took a deep breath and let the words exit his body. "Leoš created a way to stop these stupid portals showing up."

"Did he really?" she asked, eyes glistening.

"It was amazing. He finished it and we were about to test it, but Vít was totally against the idea. Then it disappeared. We think he destroyed it. Leoš confronted Vít about it." Jon bit down on his tongue. Thinking back to the day, he lost all the colour in his face. "...they started fighting. I couldn't stop it." Tears swelled in the corners of his eyes, the pain in his stomach churned again. "The blood..." With the hand he held Yalda with, he squeezed her tight, the other hand went straight to his mouth and bit down on his nails.

"Vít killed my son." It was more a statement than a question. Her voice hollow as she spoke.

Jon nodded.

"Thank you for telling me, Jon." She held him closer, like somehow she already knew. "Tell me, what was the technology Leoš created?"

"It was a device, lots of little devices that he would set around different parts of the planet. According to the calculations, when the population got too much, the devices would activate and increase the land mass."

She thought about it for a moment. "Like a planet grower?"

He laughed, wiping away his tears. "Something like that."

"And then there wouldn't be overpopulation?"

"Yep, it would never occur so the portals would never show up."

She smiled. "That sounds like my son."

"But the portals did show up." Jon felt sick looking up at the bright white column the people were stepping into—turning into light as they disappeared.

"But why? We haven't reached the point of overpopulation. We had strict birth control laws and more free land than we occupied or used." She went silent for a moment. Jon recognised the same face in Leoš just before he came up with a brilliant idea. "Do you think they were called?"

"I didn't call them," Jon said. But he knew exactly the person who would do such a thing. Jon twisted his head around but before he could look, two hands latched onto his shoulders and twisted him around.

Before he understood what had happened, something hard and solid collided against his cheek. Darkness washed over his eyelids and he hit the ground. The dense crowd surrounding them pushed him back to his feet but Jon's leg's were as solid as jelly.

Vit continued to throw blow after blow at Jon's head. Jon's eyes blurred and his legs could barely hold him up. Several men pulled Vít back, giving Jon a chance to find his feet.

"Jon!" Yalda screamed. "Get moving, you've got to run! Run!"

Jon listened and ran towards the portal. Glancing over his shoulder, he saw Vít fought off the men holding him and ran after Jon.

His legs still jelly-like, slowed his pace, but Jon was determined to reach the light. Up ahead he could taste the freedom, feel a brand new life somewhere beyond the stars. He stopped, clutching at his stomach, and coughed up blood. His tongue rolled over the new gap between his teeth, then kept going. Without looking back, he reached the first step to the portal.

Two hands shoved him from behind, and he flew through the air, skidding sideways across the ground. Vít was on top of him, raising his arms high into the air.

Jon squeezed his eyes shut waiting for the final blow.

Nothing came.

Jon opened his eyes and saw Vít being dragged off by two large guards. The guards had left their post at the portal's stairs to chase Vít down. Thrashing his legs out each way, Vít fought against them.

Yalda reached Jon's side and helped him to his feet. "My son would have been proud of what you did today."

"It wasn't enough." He looked down, sad and ashamed.

"No." She lifted his chin. "You were amazing, and I'm sorry that I won't see all the amazing things you'll do in the future."

Jon smiled and felt relief wash through his body. He no longer felt the guilt of Leoš' death. For far too long it had weighed him down, like somehow he was the reason for the death in the first place. But Jon wouldn't allow that to happen again. Injustice in his name would only be fixed with releasing the truth, not holding it in like a burdened secret.

Jon leaned in and hugged Yalda. He whispered in her ear. "See you in the future." He pulled back and winked, then turned to face the portal.

At the bottom of the steps, he looked up as he approached the portal light.

A noise behind them erupted, and Jon barely heard what was happening. Forth step up, and he twisted around, feeling a cold slither rip down his arm.

Down on the first step, Yalda was clinging onto Vít in a failed attempt to hold him back—Vít had somehow broke free from the portal guards. He lunged again at Jon, inching closer with the small knife. Jon stumbled, falling onto the stairs.

Yalda and the surrounding crowd grabbed hold of Vít and forced him back, but the man wore nothing but violence in his face. Regardless of the hands holding him back, he leaned closer to Jon.

Frantically, Jon kicked back, hitting Vít in the stomach.

Vít fell backwards, into the crowd.

With just moments to get away, Jon rolled onto his stomach, pushed himself up and climb the last remaining steps. But before he could enter the portal, Vít once again had a hold.

Standing at the doorway, Jon turned around and faced Vít. Everyone nearby paused and watched. The silence was deafening.

At Jon's throat, pressed firm against his skin, was the serrated edge of the knife.

"I warned you," Vít spat. "Don't think you'll be going to your new beginnings. Life ends for you here."

Jon knew this moment would come. He stood there waiting. He had made peace with what had happened and knew the truth would bare this consequence.

Jon looked into Vít's dark eyes. The colour drained from Vít's face. He stood tall, towering over Jon, but no longer strong enough to keep the knife firmly pressed. His arms fell to his side. The fat in his cheeks wobbled then he dropped to his knees.

Behind him, Yalda stood with a bloody knife in her hands. She had driven it into his back.

Jon smiled.

"Now forget this life, Jon," she said, dropping the knife to the ground. "Once you walk through that portal, start anew. You're a smart kid. You can change the universe." Stepping over Vít's body, she reached out and handed him something.

Jon looked at it and recognised the hard drive. "But ... is this Leoš?"

"Yes, his life's work. Now it's yours."

Jon smiled, knowing the responsibility, and held it to his chest with both hands. He took a step backwards into the portal doors, and before the light took him, he looked out to the crowd and saw his parents, grandmother and sisters for the very last time.

"This is just the beginning," he whispered and his body lifted off the ground, destined for a place somewhere in the vast galaxy.

About the author

A. A. Warne writes elaborate, strange, dark and twisted stories. In other words, speculative fiction.
Located at the bottom of the Blue Mountains in Sydney, Australia; Amanda was born an artist, grew up a painter, before going it not the study of pottery. But it wasn't until she found the art of the written word
is when her universe expanded.
A graduate of Western Sydney University in arts, Amanda now spends her time wrestling three kids and writing full time.
To keep updated on her upcoming release of Heavy Dirty Soul and The Reluctant Wizard series, or just drop her a line to say hi; head to:
AAWarne.com
Facebook.com/AAWarne
Instagram.com/AAWarne
Twitter.com/AAWarne

Remember Me

Jocelyn Spark

SHE RAN THROUGH THE trees; her breath reduced to short gasps as her feet pounded against the roughened ground. She couldn't let herself be caught—the creature was more than twice her size with teeth that could rip through her skin like soft fruit. It always surprised her, the beast's agility, she didn't see how it was possible for it to dodge and weave the way it did, yet it remained close on her heel. Nearing her trap—a hole she had spent days painstakingly digging and lining with sharpened sticks—she hoped that it was big enough for the beast that chased her. Without hesitation she leapt across the opening, landing on the other side at the same time a roar from the beast was abruptly cut off, its heavy body skewered on the stakes below.

The forest went still and quiet, a silent goodbye to the creature below. She would have plenty of food for the coming months. She was thankful the skewers had proven long enough, as she had been aiming for a smaller creature such as the syth that preyed through the trees. Their fur was soft and warm, and she could have used their two elongated front teeth in her spears and weapons. Nonetheless, a bounty such as the two-legged creature she had captured meant she would not have to hunt for some time. Whilst she couldn't use its skin to make the warm clothing she had hoped for, she could fashion strong boots and armour to help protect her against the elements.

A twig snapped nearby and she spun towards the sound, her arms poised to fight—on the other side of her trap stood another being. He was tall and dressed in syth fur. He edged closer and she took an involuntary step back. It had been many moons since she awoke in the cave, alone and naked, not knowing who she was or where she came from. She had taught herself to hunt and survive, and in that time she had never seen another like her. It felt strange to her, the concept of interaction, and she took a second step backwards. She was a solitary being. She had always been alone. Her chest contracted when her eyes settled on his face. Something about those eyes seemed familiar.

"Alora." His whisper just reached her ears. She froze and rolled the word along her tongue. He stepped closer, like he was hunting a wild beast. She felt caged.

"Alora," he pleaded.

What did Alora mean? Was that what she was called? When she had awoken in the cave her thoughts followed a natural flow. She knew the sky was up and the ground was under her hardened feet. But she was less sure of things like the beast she had just killed or the syth she'd wanted. Images of other creatures and their names were vivid in her mind, yet she had never come across a jianthen or a cressitor, and she wondered if they were creatures of her imagination.

She glanced at the beast in the hole; she could catch another. The man took another tentative step closer and she waited no longer. She turned and fled.

SEVERAL MOONS PASSED and the sun began to warm the air once more. Alora stripped off her beast armour and stepped into the frigid lake, then dived underwater. She had taken to referring to herself as Alora after the strange being used the word. She had practiced saying it out loud many times and the word now felt pleasing on her tongue. When she came up for air, Alora saw him on the edge of the lake. He hadn't noticed her. He proceeded to strip off his fur coat and step into the cool water. Like her, he must crave the feeling of cleanliness after a long, cold winter. She edged towards the bank. During the hard winter she had lost a considerable amount of weight. He had guarded the beast in her trap for days after she had escaped him, and with little time to catch another she'd found minimal pickings over the winter to nourish herself. Her tiny frame made her progress through the water easier, with minimal drag and the smallest of ripples.

He flinched as he inched deeper into the lake. Alora froze to the spot, unable to take her eyes off him. She could almost feel the heat radiate off his body. His smooth, tanned skin glowed from the last of the sun's rays. His back stiffened and he jerked his head, locking eyes with her. He broke their stare and dove below the water. Alora frowned, what was he doing? Moments later he broke the surface only a few short meters from her. She couldn't help but search out his eyes once more, the hunger behind them causing her to shiver. Once again, he broke their stare and dove beneath the water. Her stupor broke and she turned, racing for the nearby bank.

Alora leapt into action and dived into the water. She had spent many of her waking hours strengthening her body and learning to fight and fend for herself but, in the water, she struggled to find a rhythm. She pulled herself through the water, kicking desperately to get to the bank. A hand wrapped around her ankle, fear causing her to inhale the water. The hand released her and she stood, coughing, and tried to catch her breath. Before she could attempt to swim away, his large hands grabbed hold of her waist.

Alora's eyes darted towards the shore and she knew she had to act quickly. She moved closer and a frown formed on his face.

"Alora?"

She hesitated. That word—what did it mean? His hand relaxed slightly on her arm. She used the opportunity to break free and dive below the water. If she could manage to stay under for a while he would lose her amongst its shadows. She remained under water until her lungs screamed for air before breaking the lake's surface, gasping. Her feet made contact with the soft clay and she ran towards the shore. The water pulled against her legs, the drag easing with every step she took.

"Alora stop. I won't hurt you. Please. You have to remember me." She hesitated on the bank and turned towards his voice. He no longer pursued her; rather, his shoulders slumped and his hand was outstretched towards her. "It's me, Kavan."

Her back stiffened with his final word. Kavan. A large cave with glowing lights and smooth edges, flashed through her mind. It was filled with hundreds of beings just like her and Kavan. She saw him, in the same stance—his hand outstretched towards someone. Alora tried to grasp onto the memory but she couldn't make out who was reaching back for him. Was it her? The image in her mind began to dissolve, along with her consciousness. She felt her body go light and her mind go blank as she landed with a thump on the clay below.

ALORA RUBBED AT HER head, unsure how long she had been unconscious—that other being, that Kavan, must have brought her here. She shuffled against the cold wall of the cave and twisted her head from side to side, her eyes taking time to adjust to the dim light. A flickering light came from a pile of wood on the ground not far from her. It exuded a warmth she had not felt before. What was this magic? No one was in the cave with her. She scrambled to her feet and stumbled as a wave of dizziness took her. Alora fell forward, her hand landing in the flickering light.

Excruciating pain reverberated through her hand and arm where the light touched, and she screamed. Strong hands gripped her by the waist and pulled her backwards away from the heat. The skin on her hand began to bubble and blister, parts of her skin peeled back, exposing raw flesh.

"Alora. Alora, wake up. It's starting to heal. Alora!" She opened her eyes and her heart thundered in her chest. Kavan leaned over her, her body cradled gently in his lap. His eyes were fixed on hers and she couldn't help but notice the way sadness was embedded within them. Pain pulsated through her arm, shocking her out of her reverie. She leapt away from him, taking care not to go near the flickering light.

Her chest rose and fell quickly, her eyes darting between Kavan and her throbbing arm. The open wounds had begun to knit themselves together and the blisters disappeared, leaving angry red markings all the way from her fingertips to her elbow. No matter how many times she had watched herself heal, it still fascinated her.

"I know you." Alora whispered, still watching her arm return to its normal pink skin.

"You remembered?" In a heartbeat he was right in front of her, his hand soft and warm on her cheek.

She edged back against the wall and out of his reach. "Not properly. But I remember something about a big cave."

His shoulders slumped; taking a step back he slid down the cave wall and placed his head in his hands.

"Tell me then. Tell me what I don't remember."

"I can't."

"What do you mean you can't?"

"I just can't." He stood up and strode out the entrance of the cave. Alora stormed after him, anger starting to boil in the pit of her stomach. How dare this being know things about her but not tell her! She had a right to know. "You can't? Why not? Don't just walk away from me!"

"Alora, please trust me. I can't tell you. They told me if I tell you it will kill you."

A sharp pain stabbed into Alora's chest and her legs buckled beneath her. Kavan caught her before she hit the ground.

"What happened? Are you okay?"

Her chest was still too tight to respond and they stayed in the awkward embrace for several moments before Alora found the stamina to speak. "Who's they?"

"Can't you see I can't tell you anything? That pain, whatever it was, was because I said too much. Please, just trust me."

Alora tilted her head and took the time to really study him. His strong features softened and he placed her gently on the ground before moving back from her. "I would never hurt you."

Alora looked past Kavan at the jungle. It would be easy to slide away amongst its undergrowth and escape, to return to the life she had become accustomed to. She got to her feet and took one more look at the vegetation before turning and walking back inside the cave, hoping that her willingness to stay spoke louder than anything she could say.

MOONLIGHT SHONE OVER the valley. A feeling of calm filled Alora as she took in the view from her spot on the cliff. The cave behind her had become their home many moons ago. Its position kept them safe from the beasts that roamed the valley floor and the view was something to behold.

"Alora, join me by the fire." Kavan roused Alora from her thoughts and she turned to face the man she had come to know as her own. Many summers had passed since that fateful day at the lake; her arm still tingled with the memory of her first experience with fire. He had introduced her to many things since; from how to use the sun to measure time and the taste of the delicious yellow fruit that hung high in the trees. Even without her memories, she felt connected to him in a way that she couldn't explain. He never talked about their life before they met in the jungle, and she never asked. Not anymore; the pain in his eyes every time she brought it up caused her heart to constrict with guilt.

She joined Kavan by the fire near the edge of the cliff and snuggled into his embrace, looking out over their quiet valley. Over time Alora had come to realise that it was not just the gift of healing that they shared, but neither she or Kavan had aged. The beasts in the jungle lived and died but they drifted through each passing summer with no change. At first the realisation scared her, but now that she had Kavan by her side she couldn't wait to live her eternity with him.

The silence of the night was broken when Alora dared to ask a question she'd long thought about. "Do you love this me as much as you loved the old me?"

His chest vibrated and a laugh escaped his lips. She moved away from him, frowning at his reaction.

"Alora, you are still the same person, only you are unable to see. I will love you no matter how many lives we lead."

She pressed a kiss against his still smiling lips and his warm embrace engulfed her, bringing her to his lap.

"Well, isn't this a picture." The unexpected voice startled them, and they leaped up into a defensive position, facing the intruder. Before them stood a young man, his shoulders rigid and his stance wide. Not far behind him stood several cloaked figures, their stance mimicking the man in front. She stumbled back and landed on the ground as Kavan pushed her behind him, towards the entrance of the cave.

Kavan spoke before she had a chance to question him. "Leviathan, we have not broken any rules of your punishment. Leave us."

The man's face grew darker and he took a menacing step towards Kavan. "It is King Leviathan. Do not forget that."

"You are no longer my king. You lost that title when you banished us."

"And I told you what the repercussions would be if you helped Alora remember."

Alora took this moment to stand. Ignoring Kavan's outstretched arm, she pushed past him.

"He hasn't helped me. I don't know who you are. My only memories are the ones I have of this jungle."

The King frowned in confusion as he spoke, "but you love him again, yes?"

"More than I could ever have imagined possible." Who was he to question her love? Alora could not understand where these intruders came from. Seeing other beings like them didn't feel right. The cloaked figures behind the King began to whisper and shuffle their feet.

"Enough!" boomed the King. Alora could have sworn the ground shook beneath her. He turned his attention back to Kavan, pointing a finger in his direction. "You, you lie. I told you once before that love does not conquer and it will not survive. You both will perish. I will not stand for this defiance."

The ground began to rumble. This time Alora felt it tremble beneath her feet. In the moonlight, hundreds of winged beasts took to the sky, their panicked screams filling the night.

"My King, perhaps..." The cloaked figure was cut off by the King, his eyes now red with rage as he picked the cloaked figure up in his hands. A horrendous scream echoed through the night as the man imploded into a mist of dust and ash. Alora gasped and froze at such a display of power; she couldn't run even with Kavan yelling at her to move. Kavan picked her up and ran for their cave. At its entrance, he put her down before slowly turning back to face the king.

"Even in death you will not part us."

The king roared. The ground shook harder and the wind whipped painfully against their skin. "There will be nothing left of this world. There will be nothing left of you."

No longer waiting, Kavan grabbed Alora's hand and they ran inside the cave. They had explored its vast tunnels many times before—maybe they could escape. But Kavan stopped near their bed, strewn with leaves and grass.

"What are you doing? We need to run."

"We can't. We will not escape his wrath. I am sorry. I should never have come after you. I should have watched you from afar and been content to know you were safe."

"Kavan. Kavan." She repeated his name as she used a finger to lift his head, bringing his eyes to meet hers. "If dying today means that I had you in my life then that is worth more to me than a thousand summers of living without you."

Kavan and Alora reached for each other, entwining themselves together just as an explosion of noise erupted around them. The deafening noise ripped apart Alora's eardrums until there was no sound. She stared at Kavan, his lips moving, but she heard only silence. Blood tears began to stream down his face and she tasted blood as her own tears reached her mouth. A veil lifted from her mind and she saw Kavan as he once was. She choked on the blood, trying to speak the words she knew he needed to hear.

"I remember."

Alora sank into her memories of home as blackness engulfed her.

"WE DO NOT FEEL. WE do not love. We do not allow emotions to rule. Your memories will be wiped. You will be banished."

Alora's back stiffened as King Leviathan handed down the verdict. A single tear rolled down her cheek, her eyes searching out Kavan's standing only metres away. So close, yet so far. Sadness marred his handsome face, one that, surely, she reflected. Alora turned back to the council. She wanted to shout at them, beg them, plead with them. But she knew it would be fruitless. Instead, before anyone had the chance to stop her, she tore free of the guards' grasp and ran for Kavan. His arms embraced her with purpose and strength. His body shuddered as they moulded perfectly together. It was a mere second before the guards ripped her from his arms.

Kavan's deep voice echoed through the silent room. "You feel. You love. But instead of admitting such, you hide behind your lie of no emotions. Fear has weakened you. Fear is what holds you back. We are the ones who have evolved." The public display of affection was enough to send even the most forward of her people into a stupor. Kavan rarely spoke—a man of few words. An underlying trait of the Thal; why speak when you do not do so for enjoyment, but only purpose? "You will not silence the love I have for Alora. She is my soul. She is my saviour."

Gasps of shock imploded through the room. It was one thing to hear about two Thal allowing emotions to overrule them, but for one to speak it in such terms—unheard of.

"Silence," boomed the voice of the king. Quiet rumblings continued through the room until a loud crash thundered through the room as the king hit the gong. "Such views are the reasons cities have fallen. Worlds lost. Love is the creator of war. Kavan, my punishment for you has changed. You will be banished alongside Alora; however your memories intact, hers wiped. You will see that love does not conquer and it does not survive."

Mumblings began to rise once more. Insubordination was not heard of and Alora was sure those here today would feel his wraith for such murmurings. Kavan was right; the king hid behind lies of an emotionless mind. But the emotion of pride and greed were strong within his character. Thal had long lost the understanding of emotion. Their ancestors a millennium ago had ensured that.

Alora looked directly at her king and spoke with conviction, "You may take my memories but you cannot take my heart."

His eyes turned murderous, his gaze bored into hers. He once more turned his ice-cold eyes towards Kavan. "You will not aid her in regaining her memories. If you do, she will die." A slight shift in stance was the only signal he gave the ruling council. A ripple of power flowed through the room and engulfed Alora. She fought against it as she swung towards Kavan. He too, struggled against the guards, his eyes locked solely on Alora. The words he yelled were lost against the noise in her mind and the encroaching blackness.

"I will remember you." She whispered into the room.

THEY AWOKE STILL LOCKED together in each other's embrace, their bodies drenched in blood. Kavan placed his warm hand on her cheek, his eyes exploring her face before locking his gaze with hers. He inched closer until she could feel his warm breath against her neck. "You remembered me?"

Alora placed her palms against his chest and gently pushed him back. His eyes were no longer dulled by sadness, but filled with hope.

"Kavan." Her hand moved to his face, caressing his cheek. "My mind didn't need to remember you when my heart always did." She leant into his warm embrace and breathed in his familiar scent; even more intoxicating now that she remembered him and what they went through at home. Home—a term she could no longer use for a place that had banished them. This was her home. The king had not succeeded in killing them—although she was sure he had come close. The Thal had witnessed his wrath; his vengeance for dominance. They would rise against him. Her people would one day defeat King Leviathan and he would be no longer. She could only hope that they would embrace love and family above all else. One day, she hoped that more of her people would join them here and call this place home.

Kavan's breathing became a steady rhythm, slumber once again taking him. Alora almost gave into the exhaustion that flowed through her body, but she wanted to see the devastation the king had caused. She untangled herself from her beloved, careful not to wake him as she laid a gentle kiss on his blood-covered cheek. A smile crept across her face, as the thought of cleansing each other in the warm lake took root in her mind.

The smile disappeared the moment her eyes adjusted to the sunlight and she looked over the valley below. Her eyes filled with tears, her heart tightening in her chest. The tall trees, the blossoming plant life—nearly all gone. In its wake lay mangled corpses of the many beasts that had roamed the land and the vegetation that had covered the earth. Not far from where she stood lay the crushed body of a winged beast. It must have fallen from the sky during the king's attack; its long snout and razor sharp teeth crumpled and broken.

"So much destroyed, because of us," she whispered to Kavan as she heard his slow footsteps exiting the cave. She turned to face him when he made no response. His eyes were fixated on his arm. "What's wrong?"

He lifted his head and turned his gaze to meet hers. "My arm; it's not healing."

Alora rushed to his side, taking his arm into her hands. She inspected the deep cut that ran along his lower arm, the injury showing no signs of regeneration.

They both stood in silence for several moments, waiting and hoping that it would begin to heal. Spotting a jagged rock nearby, she reached out and ran her palm over it. Blood filled her hand and she quickly clenched her fist; a small cut like this would take only seconds to heal.

They both watched as she slowly opened her hand. Her heart lodged in her throat when the blood continued to flow. Mouth agape, Alora snapped her head up and stared at Kavan in shock. He took her hand and bought it to his lips, placing a kiss over her wound.

"We may have lost our immortality but we are alive. This is our second chance, the time to start our lives anew. Alora, I do not know what is to come but with you I know we will survive it. This is our new Nirvana. This can be our Paradise."

About the author

Many authors claim influence from greats such as Poe, Hemingway and Austen. But author, Jocelyn Spark, lives by the words of the greatest philosopher of all time—Dr. Seuss. According to Dr. Seuss, fantasy is a necessary ingredient in life, and, with a zest for life and enthusiasm for all things crazy, you will always find a touch of fantasy in Jocelyn's writing. Not only is Jocelyn an author, she is a teacher, mother, wife, cake decorator, failing gardener and a poor excuse of a basketballer. She is also one of the founding members of ASF and can't quite remember what it's like to have free time. But busy is better than bored. Follow her at https://www.facebook.com/JocelynSparkAuthor

The Teacup

Austin P. Sheehan

FRANZ KESSLER GAVE his teacup to Astrid, who smiled back at him before examining its contents. This was their ritual. Every morning she would whisper a word to him, over breakfast he would consider it while he sipped at his tea, and pass the teacup back to her when it was almost empty. Today he was meant to focus on the future, but his thoughts kept returning to his work.

While Astrid had a keen interest in reading tea leaves and fortune telling, Franz just did it to make her happy. The older he got, the more important his bond with his daughter became. His wife Marguerite, on the other hand, wouldn't have a bar of "that silly hocus-pocus," as she called it. She wanted Astrid to focus on finding a full-time job and a decent partner, both of which were in short supply in their village.

Seeing the exchange, Marguerite picked up her sudoku book with a huff and shuffled out of the room, shaking her head with disdain. Franz watched his wife leave, perplexed as usual by her deep-seated dislike of Astrid's harmless hobby. When Franz looked back at his daughter, her free hand covered her mouth and her face was ashen. His eyes caught hers, deep green and full of fear. Turning to the sink with trembling hands she emptied and washed the teacup. Franz joined his daughter to dry the remaining breakfast dishes, looking out the window which offered a view of their small yet well-kept front garden. A faint frost still covered the grass, the warmth of the day's sun hadn't reached them yet.

"What did you see?" he whispered, so Marguerite wouldn't overhear.

"Nothing, do-don't worry about it."

"Tell me. You know I don't believe in that stuff," Franz boasted, puffing out his chest in a mock show of bravado.

"True, nothing scares you, does it?" she answered with a slight smile. Franz shrugged, happy to again play the fearless hero from their adventures when Astrid was a child. "It was a skull I saw, pa," Astrid concluded with a sigh, looking up at her dad.

"A skull?"

"Yes. It scared me," she admitted, regaining her composure. "I panicked, thinking I'd foreseen your death. I've never seen an image so clearly before!"

"Should I be worried?" Astrid shook her head, her shoulder length blue curls bouncing gently. "Does a skull signify death though?" he continued. "I thought it meant change or something like that?"

She smiled up at him, her green eyes shining. "You've been listening to me, I see. Yes, in Tarot, the death card can mean a change of thinking from an old way into a new way," she explained, still in a whisper. "In tasseography, a skull means power and concentration, while dragons mean change and new beginnings."

"So the skull you saw means I'll have extra power and concentration today?"

Astrid responded with a quick, hesitant shrug, followed by a nod.

"That'll help with work then." He smiled, glancing at the clock on the wall. "I should be on my way. You'll be okay looking after Marge?"

"We'll be fine. But can't you do it tomorrow?" she asked, her pleading eyes looking up at him.

"No, I can't put it off. But I'll be fine, okay?" he said with what he hoped was a reassuring smile.

AFTER GIVING HIS WIFE a goodbye kiss, Franz donned his hat and left their cosy wood and stone home to his car, an old Mercedes. Glancing back, he saw Astrid waving from the doorway. Waving back, his heart sank with sorrow for her. She should be exploring the world, or at least living somewhere with career opportunities, not stuck in a small town looking after her sick mother. Still, he was glad to have her around.

The sun was still low in the sky as he drove to St Agatha's church, not far from the village of Rettenberg where the Kesslers had lived for almost sixty years. Franz was just over sixty himself and barely remembered his first few years in East Berlin or his family's escape. His parents told him stories about it though, and how they ended up coming to this village. His father wanted them to disappear amongst the crowds in a big city. His mum got her way though, as she often did.

"We don't know those cities, Wilhelm," she had said, reenacting their story to Franz one winter's night. "But we've visited Bavaria many times. Don't you remember our honeymoon in the mountains? Haven't we always talked about moving to a quiet town there one day? Well this is that day," she said, her voice firm. "And if the Stasi are hunting East German traitors like us, they'll look in the big cities first."

Franz remembered his loving parents with warmth and pride, and was ever thankful to the Kingdom of Bavaria for granting them asylum, and to the people of Rettenberg for welcoming them into their community.

OVER THE DECADES THAT Franz had lived there, he'd always enjoyed the view of the great snow-capped mountains and the tranquility of village life. But today he didn't have time to admire the scenery, he had a job to do. The church's heating system was on the fritz, and as the only repairman in the village, it fell upon him to fix it. He'd driven past St Agatha's many times; it was a white stone chapel with a square tower that had stood for centuries in the picturesque valley just out of town.

Franz parked his car by the side of the road and looked up at the charming building. He was always struck by how tiny it was, just nine pews and six stained glass windows—nothing like Munich's famous *Frauenkirche,* dominating the Bavarian capital, or even the St. Lorenz Basilica in nearby Kempten. Entering the church yard, his steel toolbox clanked with every step.

Clank. Clank. Clank.

Then he stopped.

Crunch.

Franz gaped in stunned silence at the scene before him, his toolbox lying forgotten at his feet. The normally immaculate church was covered in mud, and the perfectly manicured lawn was ruined. Two large ochre mounds of damp earth filled the churchyard, with mud and splintered pieces of wood scattered everywhere. Worst of all was the rancid smell which enveloped him, making him retch.

Pinching his nose with his fingers, he surveyed the scene, trying to pinpoint where the horrid stench was coming from. Then he saw it, sticking out of a pile of dirt. An old glove, supported by an arm. His stomach lurched. The arm's saggy, rotted skin was dark yellow with splotches of black and green. Some long-dead corpse's arm was protruding from the mound. Franz felt the sickness rising as the foul odour overpowered him. Old leather shoes overflowing with decaying flesh were strewn in the garden bed. A smashed coffin the size of a suitcase lay on the steps of the church. If he had taken one more step his foot would have landed on a jawbone—a human jawbone. He swallowed hard, bending to retrieve his toolbox, then jumped back in fright as a smashed skull stared up at him. With his heart pounding and steps faltering, Franz returned to his car, terrified and repulsed by his discovery.

With his hands trembling on the leather steering wheel, Franz searched in vain for an explanation. What could have caused such a mess? Why would anyone disturb the graves of these long-dead souls, smashing their coffins, scattering their limbs and skulls around the churchyard? His heart skipped a beat as he remembered Astrid had seen a skull in his tea leaves. He couldn't stop his mind reeling, nor could he stop his racing heart. Trying to calm down, he convinced himself that it was a mere coincidence, reading tea leaves was foolish nonsense after all. After composing himself, Franz knew he'd have to call the police. With a barely noticeable tremble, he reached for his phone.

"Good morning, this is Sergeant Dreyfuss, Rettenberg Police."

"Sergeant Dreyfuss, this is Franz Kessler," he said, his voice shaking. "The St. Agnes church has been, well, vandalised."

"Do you mean graffiti, Herr Kessler?"

"No. You should see it for yourself, Sergeant," Franz said, then hesitated before whispering, "there are smashed coffins and body parts everywhere." He waited in silence for a response, not wanting to repeat something he could scarcely believe himself.

"Stay there, Herr Kessler," said Dreyfuss, his voice crisp with urgency. "I'm on my way."

WHEN THE BLUE-AND-WHITE *Polizei* BMW arrived, Sergeant Dreyfuss emerged and walked over to where Franz still sat in his Mercedes.

"Morning Herr Kessler, how is the wife?" Dreyfuss asked. Being a policeman in a village like Rettenberg meant that no matter the circumstances, you always started with the pleasantries.

"Same as always," Franz replied, barely able to hide his impatience. "And you?"

"Can't complain," Dreyfuss answered, resting his hands on the roof of the Merc. Then, lowering his voice, "you say you've seen smashed coffins and body parts, Franz?"

"Yes, in the churchyard," nodded Franz. "I came to fix the heater, but when I got here..." His voice trailed off, unable to find the words he needed. He looked up at the Sergeant with a helpless shrug.

"Let's have a look then, Herr Kessler."

Franz followed the police officer through the gate, keeping his eyes averted from the putrefying limbs and ruined caskets that littered the scene. Dreyfuss strolled towards the mounds, unperturbed by the grisly scene, using a handkerchief to cover his nose and mouth. Franz caught up with Dreyfuss and together they looked into the deep chasm that someone or something had created.

"What do you think?" asked Franz, his voice muffled by the jumper he'd pulled above his nose to combat the rancid odour.

"Desecration. Someone's made a messy job of digging up these old graves," Dreyfuss answered through the handkerchief.

"I have to say that you don't appear surprised, Sergeant."

"To be honest, Herr Kessler, I had expected this," Dreyfuss said, locking his eyes with Franz's. "Similar scenes have occurred in other towns in and around the mountains."

"What do you mean?"

"There's always two trenches in the ground, and two mounds of earth. Always limbs and heads strewn across the churchyard. And that's all that's left, where are the rest of the bodies?" Franz glanced around, Dreyfuss was right. Whoever had done this had only left behind arms, legs and the odd skull. "But no footprints. No tyre tracks or evidence of any digging equipment. But just here," Dreyfuss continued, kneeling down between the two earthen mounds, "see how smooth it is?"

"You're right, the grass looks like it's been flattened. But I don't understand it, Sergeant. Who would do this? And for the love of God, why?"

"That I don't know," replied Dreyfuss with a shrug. "But they only target remote old churches. The nearest church like that is St Nikolaus. Do you know it?" Franz noded. "I'll keep an eye on it tonight, and if anything happens I'll let you know. I'm going to close this scene off now."

"But I haven't fixed the heater!"

"No-one's going to need it until this is all cleaned up, Franz," said Dreyfuss impatiently, pulling a card out of his shirt pocket and handing it to Franz. "I'll call when we're done. And if you need to talk to anyone about what you've seen, there's a number on the card." Franz pocketed the card, and, understanding that he'd been dismissed, returned to his car. He contemplated going home but he couldn't tell Marguerite of the horrors he'd seen, so instead he to drove into the village to run some errands while he waited for the call.

FRANZ BUSIED HIMSELF with other jobs for the rest of the morning, then went to his favourite cafe for a coffee to pass the time. Despite enjoying the wholesome earthy aromas of the dark brew in front of him, he couldn't get the images of the putrefying arms and legs out of his head. His hands sought out the card Sergeant Dreyfuss had given him, and he tapped it rhythmically on the wooden table. What disturbed Franz even more than the images was the mystery surrounding it all, not knowing who had done it, why they'd left the limbs and taken the bodies, or what had driven them to commit such desecration. Closing his eyes to try to piece it together, he saw the crushed skull underneath his toolbox, and his heart lurched, again recalling that Astrid had seen a skull in his tea leaves. Had she foreseen this? He had a nagging feeling that there must be some connection, as ridiculous as it sounded. Remembering how she'd asked him to stay home, he slammed the card down on the table - she must have foreseen it! Franz jerked to his feet and left the cafe, determined to return home and talk to his daughter. As he reached the Mercedes, his phone rang. Sergeant Dreyfuss.

"Good afternoon, Franz here" he answered.

"Herr Kessler? This is Sergeant Dreyfuss. We're done at the church so you can come back and fix the heater when you're ready."

"I'm on my way." Franz hung up with a sigh. Work first, as always.

"HELLO FRANZ," MARGUERITE said, smiling as she struggled out of her seat to greet him.

"Hello dear. Where's Astrid?" He kissed her on the cheek and looked around the room for their daughter.

"Oh, the restaurant asked her to go in early. One of her colleagues must be sick."

"And you're okay?" he asked, concealing his disappointment.

"Yes, much better now you're home."

Franz nodded and walked past her to the bathroom for a shower, determined to scrub his body clean of any trace of the lingering scent. If he could scrub the images of the rotting flesh from where they had been etched into his retinas, he would have done that, too.

"You seem quiet," observed Marguerite over dinner.

"I was thinking about Astrid," he answered. "Sometimes I think she should be working or studying in the city instead of being cooped up here looking after us."

"So..." Marguerite nodded.

Franz sat in silence waiting for her to continue. Words didn't always come easily to her since the accident, and he regretted raising the issue again.

"So," she repeated, "you are right, but is she not happy? Do we not need her?"

This time it was his turn to nod.

"She does seem happy enough, and we'd struggle without her. I can't deny that."

"I worry how we would cope without her," Marguerite said, her concern clear in her trembling voice. "And I want to keep watch on her. I don't approve of her witchcraft nonsense. If she's happy, let us all be content."

After retiring to bed, Franz still couldn't forget the horrible images and the overpowering stench of the rotting flesh, nor could he stop wondering what was behind it. Tossing and turning, his thoughts returned to Dreyfuss' notion that whatever happened at St Agatha's last night might happen at St Nikolaus' tonight. Hours of futile attempts to sleep passed before he accepted that it was hopeless. He kissed his sleeping wife on the cheek and crept out of the house.

The moon was obscured by clouds as Franz drove north through the quiet streets of Rettenberg, then through the empty countryside to the valley where St Nikolaus stood—another tiny church in the middle of nowhere. He parked far enough away that his approach would go unnoticed. Trying to make as little noise as possible, he trudged up the steep hill. The tall church tower stood out black against the cloudy sky, and his stomach churned with a sense of wrongness. A deep growl rumbled through the night as Franz reached the gate, deep and dark, unlike anything he'd heard before. Fighting against every instinct he possessed that told him to turn and run, he darted to the arched stone doorway of the church and breathed deeply, trying to calm his racing heart.

A blood curdling scream filled the darkness. With his heart hammering in his chest, Franz peered around the wall to see Sergeant Dreyfuss standing motionless, his gun pointing into the inky blackness above him.

Bang.

Bang.

The gunshots echoed through the valley, deafening Franz who dropped to his knees. Looking up, he watched in horror as a pair of immense reptilian jaws—a dark red cavernous mouth dripping with saliva and full of pale yellow teeth as long as steak knives—descended on the Sergeant. It engulfed his torso, muffling his cries, and lifted him off the ground. With a clear snap, Dreyfuss' legs fell onto the sodden and now bloody ground.

Franz wanted to run. He wanted to hide. But he held his breath, counted to three, and again peered around the side of the church. What had he seen? What were those massive jaws attached to? Did he want to know? He had to.

The cloud had drifted, allowing the pale moonlight to shine down into the valley. The small copse of trees beyond the low stone fence was visible, as were the bloodied remains of Dreyfuss' legs. In the centre of the churchyard was a great dark writhing shape covered in scales and irregular spines. Frozen with fear, Franz's mind reeled and his heart faltered. What could it be? A massive serpent? No, it was too big, even for that. The colossal beast moved towards the stone fence and, resting on its belly, used a pair of muscular legs to dig into the ground, scooping up piles of earth on both sides of its body. A pair of large bat-like wings adorned the scaly body, looking too frail and small to support the weight of the massive creature.

Franz' heart was racing, his stomach had turned to ice, and all he wanted to do was run. Yet he couldn't take his eyes off this behemoth. He had only one word to describe this creature. But it was impossible, it couldn't be a dragon. He crouched, frozen in fear as the monster's massive head rose into the air, craned to the left and sniffed at the mound it had created. Franz saw its elongated face, the thick metre-long snout covered with ridges. But his attention was focused on the creature's large circular eyes. With a deep growl, it bit into the mound of earth, and when it drew its head back, a pair of emaciated, skeletal legs, tattered trousers and deteriorated leather shoes dangled from its mouth. A second later, they fell to the ground and Franz watched in disgust as the monster's throat convulsed, swallowing the putrid remains whole. When it turned its head to examine the other pile, Franz ducked back out of sight.

Without hesitating, Franz sprinted through the gate, then retraced his steps down the hill, one at a time. Pausing for breath, he felt the hairs on the back of his neck stand on end, an icy chill ran up his spine. He felt the monster's eyes watching him. Franz took one step, then another. When he put his foot down for the third time, he tripped and crashed to the ground, gasping for air. A deafening roar sounded behind him, and Franz was on his feet again, pumping his legs harder than at any point in his last thirty years, perhaps ever. His chest was burning and his legs were aching. A loud rumble and scrape of movement was just behind him, and he thought each moment would be his last. The memories of those massive jaws engulfing Sergeant Dreyfuss pushed him on, and he thought he had a chance when his car came into view. Giving thanks that he hadn't locked it, Franz jumped behind the wheel and started the car.

The headlights came on, shining up the hill—right into the face of the pursuing beast. The dragon was heading straight for the Mercedes, sliding along the ground and propelling itself using its two muscular legs. Blinded and confused by both the headlights and the roar of the engine as the car burst to life, the beast veered to the left. Seizing the chance, Franz stamped down hard on the accelerator and swung the steering wheel in the opposite direction. Looking out the car's windows, Franz saw nothing but darkness as he sped away.

Over the deep growl of the German engine, Franz heard a frustrated roar somewhere behind him. Panicked, he turned his headlights off, hoping the darkness might hide him from the pursuing beast. Using the moonlight to guide him, he drove through the valley, then veered erratically back and forth through the empty streets of the village, making sure it couldn't follow him home. Yet no matter what he did, he felt hunted, constantly sensing movement just outside his field of vision, and hearing otherworldly growls and the flapping of wings.

WHEN FRANZ RETURNED home, he was breathless, shaking, and covered in sweat. The house was dark—both Astrid and Marguerite would be fast asleep. Good. Franz looked out the windows but could see only darkness. But he knew it was still out there. Even now it might be following his trail, despite his attempts to confuse it. Maybe the heat from his car's engine or the smell of its exhaust could lead the dragon to his home, to his family. Sleep would not be an option tonight, or any night soon. Franz no longer doubted that the massive two-legged, winged reptilian beast was a dragon. It had eaten the Sergeant, dug up and consumed human remains from the church's graveyard, and he had barely escaped from its jaws. Pacing back and forth, he considered what to do next. Could he go to the police? No, he wasn't going back out there tonight. Could he call them? What could he say that they'd believe? Franz entered the kitchen to make himself a cup of tea. He needed to calm down. He needed to think.

They would find Dreyfuss' legs. Then they'd comb the area, find his own footprints, his tyre tracks, and come knocking on his door. Franz didn't want to have to explain how a monstrous dragon ate a police officer. But more importantly, he didn't want his family to spend another night amongst dragon-infested mountains. Casting his eyes around the room, he saw their meagre possessions, their few heirlooms. They could pack their whole lives up into the back of the car, rent a trailer for their clothes and furniture, and find a place in a new city. Any city would do as long as it was well away from these mountains, though Nuremberg with its medieval walls would do nicely. Franz reached for his teacup as the kettle boiled, recalling his conversation with Astrid that morning. This time it was his hands that trembled as it came back to him. They'd talked about skulls, about death, about change—how much of this had Astrid foreseen? But there was something else. Dragons! The teacup spilled out of Franz' shaking hands, bouncing from the counter and smashing onto the floor. Astrid had said something about dragons—but what? As hard as he tried, it wouldn't come back to him. Kneeling down to scoop up the shattered china pieces, Franz thought about what he'd say to convince his family to move to a new city. It wouldn't be easy, but he'd find a way. After that he'd have plenty of time to ask Astrid about dragons and tea leaves. Maybe there was something to be said for all her hocus pocus after all.

About the author

Austin P Sheehan is a writer of speculative fiction, a lover of language, literature and '90s TV.

Armed with a psychology degree, he went out into the world to further study humanity, and now prefers the company of his greyhounds.

He grew up in the valleys of Victoria's high country, and despite living in Melbourne for the past decade, he always feels at home amongst the mountains. In fact you'll often find mountains in his stories, whether they're sci-fi, fantasy or alternative history.

Austin has also been getting coffees and doing photocopying as the work experience kid at the Aussie Speculative Fiction group.

If you want to discover what secrets are hidden in the mountains, go to austinpsheehanau.blogspot.com www.facebook.com/APSheehanAU or find him on twitter @AustinPSheehan

Next Journey

Chris Foley

I'M AWAKE, BUT THAT can't be right. I'm dead. Better keep my eyes closed, and maybe oblivion will reassert itself.

Hmm. I don't hear my choirs of angels gently welcoming me into the afterlife. Just a hubbub of voices rising around me. CAN'T A MAN BE LEFT TO HIS DEATH IN PEACE!

Sighing, I finally succumb to the inevitable and open my eyes. Blinking against the bright light, I sit up and stretch my cramped limbs. I've been lying on a hard bench. Looking around, I see that I'm in some giant room, like an aircraft hangar. A large crowd of people are milling around me—old, young, male, female, Caucasian, Asian, African. It feels like I'm at a cross-road of humanity.

The noise level increases as more people drift in. Some are clearly in good spirits, laughing and slapping each other on the back. Others are screaming hysterically whilst their companions try to settle them. Standing around the walls are individuals looking bewildered. There is a weird mix of clothing, as if I've woken up in the middle of a huge costume party. Pyjama-clad people mingle with those in suits; beach attire with sporting wear. It's all very confusing.

I'm wearing pyjamas too. My wish to die in bed must have been granted.

"May I sit down?" I look up to see a middle-aged man dressed in a white shirt and a pair of navy-blue trousers; dark hair with grey tinges; a little puffy around the face. An ordinary looking man— it's reassuring to meet someone just like me.

"Yeah, sure." I shift along the bench. With so many people gathering, I felt it rude of me to take up so much space.

"It's not what you expected, is it?" the man chats amiably. "This..." He gestures around the room in response to my evident confusion.

"Er, is this the afterlife?"

"A bit disappointing, really. Everyone expected to be *somewhere*, or not. But I hear there has been a bit of a snafu. The celestial forces are having trouble processing the backlog. This is the waiting room for the afterlife."

Waiting room? Snafu? Disgraceful! The product disclaimer said nothing about the possibility of 'processing backlogs'.

"My name is Phil, by the way. Phil Caruthers. I was a liner captain." He motions with his left arm over which his captain's jacket is slung. "Southampton to Athens via Lisbon, Gibraltar, and Malta. Heart attack caught me on the bridge. And you?"

His matter of fact style is calming. Death is about being calm, isn't it? "Oh, um, Smith. Rob Smith," I shake his proffered hand. "Insurance clerk. I died in my sleep, in accordance with the death package I'd taken out with my life insurance. *"Take the stress out of death"* was the sales pitch. You could decide on the manner of your death, whether you would be surrounded by loved ones, what type of afterlife you wanted and so on. I chose the 'Sublime Death' package. A quiet death in bed to be awakened in the afterlife by choirs of angels. I sold quite a few of them myself."

"Sweet."

"Mind if I join you?" A large woman with big hair, big teeth and wild orange hair squeezes onto the bench beside me without waiting for a reply. Phil and I shift further along the bench.

I should complain to someone. Or get into a queue and get 'processed', or something. My policy was all paid up. I shouldn't have to wait.

"Say, is there anyone we can speak to, Saint Peter perhaps? Buddha?" I hastily add the last suggestion. If we're in a waiting room, perhaps it's an ecumenical waiting room. "Do you know how long we have to wait for, well, whatever happens on the other side?"

"You could try that guy over there." Phil points to a seven-foot-tall, pale green skinned person, dressed in a silver-hued morning suit with a crowd of people hovering around him, shouting and pushing each other aside to get his attention. He appears to be guarding a door-shaped black-void behind him; a swishing tail keeps the doorway clear of trespassers. An assistant chivvies the crowd into a queue. "He's called the Portal Guardian."

I look around for an information desk, a 'Traveler's Help' sign or something. But I can't see anything. With a shrug, I step forward to join the queue. Standing in a queue elevates my anxieties a little.

"I'm sorry, sir," I hear the Guardian reply to a red-faced man at the front of the crush "Are you on the list?" I don't hear the man's response over the noise of the other impatient people, but the Guardian continues in a firm manner. "Until the celestial blockage is cleared, we can only let people through with pre-bookings." The Guardian turns to speak to a very prim looking short woman, next in line. Satisfied that the woman is listed on the clipboard in his hand, he issues her a pass. With a self-satisfied smirk to the red-faced man, the woman steps past the Guardian and vanishes into the void. Seeing his chance, the red-faced man makes a dash for the void but the Guardian's tail lashes out, sparks flying. The man falls to the floor, stunned. The assistant scurries over and rolls the unconscious man aside.

Time passes. A few more people are waved through to the portal and vanish into the void. Many more people are turned away.

"Name, sir?" It's my turn.

"Smith. Mr Rob Smith. Robert Aloysius Smith." I feel I'm on familiar ground; Death is really another form of bureaucracy. I used to excel in insurance bureaucracy, so surely, I can master death. "Insurance clerk. My date of birth is eleventh of June...."

The Guardian flicks through pages of his clipboard as I speak. "Smit, Smith, Smith... Smith with an 'e' or without an 'e'...? Oh yes, I have you here," his voice purrs. "Which box did you tick?"

"Uh, box?"

"Yes, on the form. Unfortunately, with the celestial blockage only your name details from your death form has come through. Normally you would expect to pass straight through from life to the afterlife of your choice, as per your wishes on the form that you completed. But not today, I'm afraid. We're trying to clear the backlog as quickly as possible. Did you tick a 'Faith' on the form?"

"Um."

The Guardian's green forehead wrinkles with exasperation. "Did you pick a religion, agnosticism or atheism? If you picked either a religion or atheism, then it's all quite simple. We give you the relevant pass and off you go."

"Um." I'm thinking madly. I wasn't particularly religious in life, but I remember that religious faith was a common box to tick on forms, and I'd completed quite a few forms in my life. What did I mark on my death form?

"You did tick a box, didn't you sir?" The Guardian speaks with exaggerated politeness. "Please, don't tell me you ticked agnosticism. With the current blockage, that will take ages to sort out."

I picture the form. I remember the boxes. My pen had hovered over Roman Catholicism. I was raised Catholic and went to church every Sunday but I decided that when I died I should finally be honest with myself. I didn't really believe. I'd considered ticking atheism but Sister Theresa in fourth grade had drilled into me fears of all manner of calamities that would befall atheists in the afterlife. Agnostics had been the pet evil of Brother Michael a few years later. So, both atheism and agnosticism were out.

I'd browsed the other options. If I wasn't going to claim Catholicism, I could hardly claim Anglicanism or any other

Christian faith; It felt hypocritical. Not knowing much about Hinduism and Buddhism, they were out too.

"I'm a..a..a Trans-Galactic Traveler!" Yes, I ticked that box. "And proud of it!" I'd spent a while completing the form, pondering different choices offered by the package, but that religion had caught my eye. I knew nothing about it, but I'd watched a lot of Star Trek episodes in my time. Perhaps their afterlife would be like some eternal cosplay convention.

"Indeed sir. Congratulations," the Guardian cried with relief. "We don't get many of your faith through here. Here is your pass. Off you go and enjoy your afterlife."

I take the proffered plastic disk and step forward. I have no idea what is to happen, but at least I seem to be going somewhere. I look around nervously for the swishing tail, but it's curled demurely at the Guardian's feet. Already he's speaking to the next person in the queue behind me. Anxiety and anticipation wrestle for dominance in my stomach, but I pause in mid-step towards the void, remembering my companion. "Hey, Phil. I've got my pass...." Phil isn't anywhere to be seen. I walk back to the bench.

"Have you seen my friend, Phil?" I ask the large woman. "You see, I've got my pass..."

"You just missed him. He joined the second queue that's opened. I told him to go on ahead. I'm waiting for the crowd to clear a bit before I get up."

Spying Phil's jacket lying abandoned on the bench, I grab it and hurry back to the portal. "Hey, Phil, I've got your jacket." I see Phil being issued a pass by the Guardian processing the second queue. He turns at my voice, and waves. "Don't worry about it. I'm an atheist. I don't need anything where I'm going. I'm off into the great oblivion. Wish me luck!" He then turns and walks through the portal.

Suddenly, I feel very alone in the middle of the jostling crowd. We'd known each other for just a few moments but Phil and I had shared some of our earliest moments post-death together. I'd felt a bond forming between us.

"Sir, you're holding up the line." It's the Guardian. His tail starts to twitch.

"Oh, sorry." I step forward into the Portal and into the inky blackness, wondering how much odder my death could get.

I'M STANDING IN A WELL-lit corridor trying to get my bearings. I feel a faint vibration through the floor. A Jamaican rhythm plays somewhere nearby.

"Good morning, sir. A pleasure to have you aboard. May I help you with your jacket? It's important to set a good example to the passengers."

"Oh, yes. Of course." Instinctively I accept assistance from the tall, middle-aged man in a white sailor's uniform who has appeared at my elbow. This must be how they greet all new Trans-Galactic Traveler arrivals. I slip into the jacket and do up the buttons. It's a double-breasted jacket and it takes a moment for me to get the buttons just right. It's a little tight but bearable.

"Splendid, sir. I'm Spacer Jones, at your service." The man stands to attention and clicks his heels, the perfect image from a navy recruitment poster. "May I lead you to the bridge?"

"Ur, bridge?" I feel events have gotten out of control. Again. I realise I'm wearing Phil's captain jacket over my pyjamas. Four gold rank bands at the jacket cuffs. "Hey, I'm not a cap ..."

Jones is already striding his way down the hallway. I race to catch-up. "I think there's been a mistake ..."

"Yes, the celestial blockage has caused problems all round. I've been on the blower to the Guardians all night trying to get updates. We've a schedule to keep. It's tremendous relief that you've come aboard, sir."

We come to a ladder. Jones shimmies up it like a monkey. I struggle a little. I haven't been to the gym in a while. Jones doesn't wait for me. Along another hallway and up another ladder. I pass other passengers. I try not to catch their eye as I hurry past. I'm puffing when I catch up with Jones again.

"Oh, Captain. Finally! Most distressing for the memsahib to be made to wait. She's been waiting simply ages for this trip." The speaker is an elderly gentleman with a pencil-thin moustache and wearing a three-piece suit with a silk cravat stuffed into the breast pocket. "Appalling inefficiency, I say." Beside him stands an elderly woman, evidently his wife, making shushing gestures to him. A Hawaiian lei hangs about her jowly neck.

"I'm not..."

Jones speaks over me before I can finish. "The Captain apologises for any inconvenience, sir. We'll be departing shortly."

Jones hustles me along and out of earshot of the irate passenger and finally we reach a hatchway into a compartment at the end of the hallway. Stepping through the hatchway, I'm drawn into a darkened space. A cold knot forms in my stomach. Have I walked through another portal and into yet another confusing form of an afterlife? After a few moments, my eyes adjust to the darkness and I realise that there are twinkling lights hovering before me. The night-sky! The clarity astounds me. I see galaxies and solitary stars arrayed. Mesmerised, I stand rooted to the spot. Craning my neck, I see still more stars above me stretching out to infinity. I'm used to seeing the night-sky through a veil of urban smog. It takes me a few moments to re-order my senses. Around me there are console stations, all lit up by their different systems. I must be on the bridge.

"Here we are, sir. Please take your seat." I'm guided to the centre seat; a large, padded chair with armrests raised above the other console stations.

"Now slow down," I finally get out. "This has gone too far. I'm not the captain of whatever it is that we're on. I'm not even a captain. This jacket," I gesture to the jacket I'm wearing which proclaims its captain's rank at the cuffs, "is not my jacket. It belonged to somebody I met at the waiting room to the afterlife. I don't know where I am. All I know is that I'm dead and I'm supposed to be in the afterlife. This seems more like the makings of a Caribbean Cruise!"

"I know that. You know that. But nobody else aboard does. This is the afterlife. We Galactic Travelers get to journey the universe upon our death. An eternal holiday if you will. Telling people that there isn't a captain aboard will just spoil it for everyone. You can't have a galactic cruise without a ship, and a ship cannot be without a captain. You happened to come along just when the passengers were getting a little restless from waiting. Trust me, it'll all be okay."

"But I know nothing about flying spaceships, planes or navigating ships. I'm an insurance clerk. I know forms, premiums and claims. You do it. You surely know more than I do."

"I don't actually. I was an investment banker. This," he plucks at his sailor's blouse, "is a costume. I paid rather lot of money for it to wear to a party, it suits me rather well, don't you think? Anyway, I got drunk, fell off the balcony and woke up here. On my reflection, I'd died pretty much the way I'd lived: a pain in the arse. Passengers started asked me questions thinking that I'm a member of the crew, and it felt good to help people. For a change. So, I decided to go with the flow. I reasoned that somebody would be along eventually to take charge."

I contemplate my situation. What's the worst thing that could happen? We're all dead anyway.

"Ok. I'll do it. What do I do?"

"There are lots of flashing lights here, but most of the real work can be done from the console in front of you. That button," Jones points to a large green button, "starts the ship—"

I push the green button. I hear an angry beeping sound from the console.

"—which I did earlier to get the engines warmed up."

"Oh, sorry." I let the button go. The beeping stops.

"The red button stops the ship. Fast." Jones seizes my hand as I reach out to touch that button too.

"Oh, sorry." It looks easier than driving a car, but I have a niggling feeling that there should be something else. "How do I, like, steer the ship? Isn't space a three-dimensional thingy? You know, up, down, left, right."

"Oh, yeah. You might want to know that. The dials..." He points to four dials, laid out in a cross pattern on the console in front of me. I peer at the labels. *Top Engine. Bottom Engine. Port Engine. Starboard Engine.* "They allow you to increase or decrease the speed of individual engines. That gives us forward momentum and allows you to steer."

Ugh?

"If you want to go forward at a steady speed, set all engines to the same speed. If you want a course change—say, you want to turn to port, turn the top and bottom engines to zero, slow the port engine whilst increasing the speed of the starboard engine. The forward momentum of the starboard engine, without the counter-balance offered by the port engine, will slew the ship around to port. Simply re-adjust the respective speed of all the engines when you've completed the maneuver."

Ugh?

"Don't worry, you'll pick it up. Let's shove off and you'll get the hang of it."

"How do you know all this?"

"I read the manual. I had time to kill before someone came aboard to take charge."

Jones was already speaking into the ship's loudspeaker before I could stop him. "Attention, ladies and gentlemen. On behalf of the Church of Trans-Galactic Travelers, I wish to apologise for the delay. We will be on our way shortly on our grand tour of the marvels of the universe. Just sit back, put your feet up, and let all the cares of your old life slip away. All external hatch-ways are now closing."

Jones signs off and stands waiting.

"Uh. What happens now?"

"You push that button." Jones point to a black button located at the bottom of the console. "That closes up the ship."

I hesitate. Pushing the button seems to signify an irrevocable step. I shrug my shoulders. It's not as if there is anything else I should be doing. I'm dead after all. I push the button.

Nothing appears to happen, but Jones appears satisfied, so I'm satisfied.

"Well done, sir. Now with two hands, take hold of the left and right engine dials," the ship lurches violently as I do so. I clutch at the armrests to keep myself from falling to the deck. Jones wasn't so lucky. He grimaces as he picks himself up. "Slowly, and evenly, turn the dials."

Perspiration starts to form on my forehead. I didn't think death could be so hard. I concentrate. I get the hang of turning the dials slowly and in unison. I feel the faint vibration that I first heard upon boarding the ship increase. The engines must be powering us forward.

I look up to see the star patterns around me shift slightly as the ship moves forward. "How fast can we go?"

"Not sure. Give it a go. We've got all the time in the universe."

Remembering the violent lurching experience when I first started to turn the dials, I turn the port and starboard dials gingerly until they reach their maximum. I then take hold of the top and bottom dial. I look up to Jones for reassurance, who nods back. I turn those remaining dials steadily and evenly until they too have reached maximum.

The star patterns around me blur into white streaks.

I let go of the dials and sit up straight. Pride surges through me. I've done it! I've put the pedal to the metal of the Great Space Liner to the Stars.

The rest of my afterlife awaits.

About the author

Chris writes stories about what ifs…what if a dead man finds himself in a queue to get into the afterlife…what if ill-considered choices on bureaucratic forms during one's lifetime pre-determine the afterlife that we get to experience…. When he isn't writing science fiction, science fantasy and historical fiction, Chris is the former founding Chair of the Historical Novel Society Australasia and is active in the fostering of the writer's craft and fellowship amongst authors. Follow him on Facebook: @ChrisFoleyAuthor

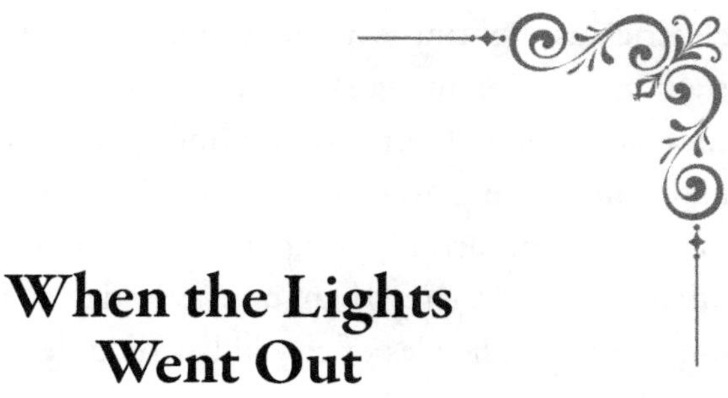

When the Lights
Went Out

Lachlan Walter

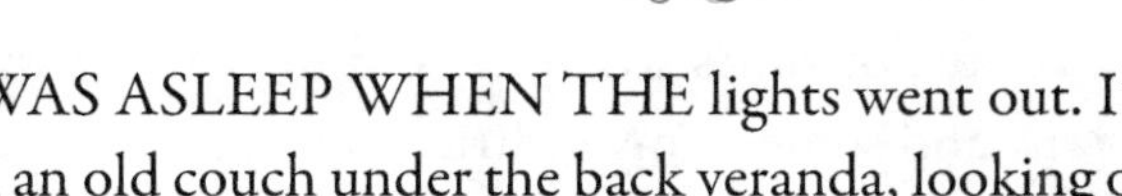

I WAS ASLEEP WHEN THE lights went out. I'd been sitting on an old couch under the back veranda, looking over the valley. The vast spread of dark bush and the rolling grassland shimmered in the moonlight and a crazy swirl of colour brightened the valley's furthest edge. Summer was at its peak and it was hot and stuffy in the house, and Will's snoring was getting to me—it was always worse in the heat and he sounded like he was roaring. And so I'd taken myself out to get some fresh air and some peace and quiet.

Actually, it wasn't really that quiet out there.

A couple of days earlier, all those city kids had made their annual trek to the abandoned farm across the valley for an outdoor techno-party. They called it a "bush doof," and they'd been doing it for years. I'd practically grown up with it and pretty much knew the routine by heart. All through January, more and more people would turn up at the abandoned farm and start turning it into a party site. Organisers, installation artists, electricians, lighting experts, sound engineers, carpenters and tradies; they spent weeks erecting massive stages and laying sprawling dance floors, assembling gargantuan sound systems and constructing towering installations and stringing up all manner of colourful lighting. If it flashed or blinked or swirled or spun, it was there. Then, on the Friday of the Australia Day long weekend, hordes of city kids would descend on it and the music would start and it was party time.

At least, it was party time for them.

When I was a kid, I'd only been able to watch them transform the abandoned farm either before school or after school, and only if I'd finished my chores and my homework. As a teen, I'd snuck out a couple of times when the old man was passed out drunk, and me and some of my girlfriends had tried to talk our way into the party, always unsuccessfully. But after I finished high school, just before the lights went out, I'd started hanging out at the farm a bit—whenever the old man let me knock off early. I'd talk shit with some of the guys and girls getting the place ready for a party—they weren't bad people, no matter what some of the locals said.

But then I'd have to go home to the old man and Will and to the thought of another day of drudgery. Even though Will and I were no longer children, the old man still liked to crack the whip on our backs. He'd tell us that what we were doing was for the good of the country; that the troops still needed to eat; that we should be thankful for having a job; that we should be hardworking and upstanding, unlike "that lot," and that if we didn't like how he did things, then we were welcome to hit the road.

And then he'd open another bottle.

All the while, "that lot"—the guys and girls getting the place ready for a party—stayed there at the abandoned farm, laughing it up, hanging out and having a great time.

At least some people were still able to enjoy themselves.

ANYWAY, SO THERE I was, sitting under the back veranda and looking over the valley. The old man was out somewhere on another bender, and like I said, it was too hot in the house and Will was snoring loud enough to shake the foundations. I liked it out there, too. I liked how the dark bush and the shimmering grassland made the awful state of the world and all the horror and war seem somehow insignificant.

When I sat there all alone and looked at it properly, I felt like everything would be okay.

Truth be told, that night I wasn't really looking at it. I was actually asleep. For an hour or so I'd been entertained by the coloured spotlights shining up into the trees, the projected laser-patterns that danced over the ramshackle tent village and the strings of blinking bulbs wound through the immense industrial sculptures and the towering Eucalypts dotted around the party site. But it had been a long day, and at some point I'd drifted off without really knowing it.

I woke with a start, convinced that something was just *wrong*.

I looked back and forth and saw nothing but dark bush and shimmering grassland, same as it ever was. I lay my head back and looked at the stars. It slowly dawned on me just how quiet it was, quiet enough that I could hear the wind moaning and branches creaking and mozzies buzzing and night-birds calling. And then it hit me – the doof-doof-doof beat that had been endlessly thumping in the background had finally stopped.

The party was over.

And then I remembered that it was only Saturday night and that the party still had days to run. I looked over the land again, and saw that the crazy swirl of bright colour that had been at the valley's furthest edge had vanished, that the lights of the party had gone dark, that the swirling rainbow mess had disappeared.

Muffled words rode on the wind, the party-people's cries reduced to faintly whispered and rather bizarre non-sequitors:

"...happened?"

"What's going..."

"...out the lights..."

"...on..."

"Don't touch..."

"...me the torch..."

I looked up at the darkened floodlight attached to the veranda wall, and I couldn't remember whether or not I'd turned it on before settling in for the night. I got to my feet and flicked the switch. Nothing. I flicked the switch a few more times. Still nothing. It could have just been dead, knowing the state of the place, but I had to be sure.

I fumbled my way into the house, my hands outstretched and grasping, and tried every light in the kitchen. Nothing. I found a torch under the sink and flicked it on. Nothing.

I drifted from room to room, carefully and slowly, feeling my way through the darkness. I tried every light in the dining room, in the lounge room, in the hallway, in the laundry and the toilet and in my bedroom. Nothing happened. I drifted some more; I threw open the fridge, tried boiling the kettle, played with the remote controls hoping the television would come on, tried to boot up the computer, and flicked lamps on and off. Once again, nothing happened.

I felt my way to the kitchen and fumbled beneath the sink, finally pulling out a hand-wound portable radio. I turned it on. Nothing, not even static. I cranked the handle a half dozen times. Still nothing. Something was definitely wrong – the power might have been out in town, but it was a bit weird if it was out across the whole country. That *couldn't* happen.

The dead radio in my hand told me otherwise. Even so, I cranked it again. Nothing.

I stopped outside Will's door and banged on it.

"Wake up, bro. Something's going on."

No reply. All I could hear was his vicious snore, and so I banged again.

"Come on, bro."

Still no reply. I gave up on being polite, threw the door open and strode in. I could just make him out, the moonlight streaming in through the curtain-less window. Up close, his snore was horrible, like the grinding of some run-down organic machine.

"Bro!" I yelled through cupped hands.

He still didn't wake up; it was almost unbelievable. And so I grabbed him by the shoulder and gave him a good shove.

"Ugh... Wha? What is it? What do you want?"

I laughed at his sleep-thickened surprise, and then met his eye. I must have looked worried, because he snapped-to straight away.

"What is it, sis? What's wrong? Is the old man home?"

I smiled at his concern, and then shook my head.

"No, I reckon he's still out there somewhere with all the other old drunks. The power's out, that's all. And the party's gone dead, too."

He raised his eyebrows and smiled widely, unaware that he was doing so.

"Really? I thought those freaks had generators and shit, so that the party would never stop. I wonder what they'll do now that the lights are out? How are they going to cut up their drugs or paint their faces or put together an awfully-fucking-ugly costume?"

"Ha ha, dickhead. They're people too, you should feel a bit sorry for them – they've probably no idea what's going on or what to do, stuck out there with no power."

He rubbed his thumb and forefinger together, playing the world's smallest violin.

"Yeah, yeah, little sister, you keep telling yourself that. They're freaks, and that's all there is to it."

"Whatever..."

Our code-word for agreeing to disagree.

"What should we do about the power?" I asked, somewhat stupidly.

"Well, there's nothing we really can do."

He reached over to the bedside table and started fumbling for his glasses. He slipped them on, and then looked down his nose at me, which was quite an achievement, considering that he was lying in bed while I was standing over him.

"You see, out there are these things that people call coal mines," he said, taking the piss. "And that's where other people dig up this hard, black stuff called coal..."

"Yeah, right-oh, give it a rest."

"And there you go, you've answered your own question."

I turned to walk out on him, and then I remembered the torch.

"The torch wasn't working either," I said, turning back. "Don't you think that's weird?"

"Not really. One of us probably forgot to replace the batteries, that's all."

"But..."

"Look, Sis – I'm not about to go traipsing around in the dark at..."

He looked back and forth, as if trying to find a clock that wasn't there.

"What time is it, anyway?" he asked.

I looked at my wrist, at the cheap digital piece-of-shit that passed as my watch, and saw that it had stopped. I felt a chill run through me – I'd only replaced the battery a couple of days earlier.

"I don't know, my watch isn't working either."

I really started to worry then. Will must have seen a twinge of panic in me, because he did his best to smile and reassure me.

"It's probably nothing, Sis. You know how it goes – we're always getting by on the rag, the old man's either too pissed or too hungover to fix anything properly or replace anything that falls apart, and we both work too much to bother thinking about what else needs doing. I mean, everything's fucking held together with spit, string and barbed wire. And as for the power going out, well, it wouldn't be the first time that the old man forgot to pay the bill. We've had blackouts before, let's just hope they don't keep on or start rolling again."

Some reassurance.

"Anyway, it's the middle of the night. Whatever's happened won't turn into hell-on-earth if you wait til sunup before checking it out."

"Yeah, alright."

"Okay then. Well, I'm going back to sleep."

"No worries," I said.

He looked me in the eye.

"So, um, you can leave."

"Oh, right, right."

WILL HADN'T COMPLETELY convinced me, but he still made a certain amount of sense. Although how I was going to get to sleep was beyond me, keyed up as I was. And so I drifted around the house some more, futilely trying those few appliances I'd overlooked.

After a while, I remembered that we had some candles stashed in the kitchen cupboard.

I dragged them out and placed a couple around the kitchen and the dining room and set them alight, and then carried one to my bedroom. I threw the door open; it was pitch black in there, the curtains drawn tight. I hurried over and opened them, balanced the candle on my bedside table, and started hunting for my phone. It wasn't something that I always carried with me

– we lived so deep in the bush that a good signal was as rare as tits on a bull – and so it took me a while to find it.

I flicked it on but nothing happened.

Without power, I had no way of knowing if it wasn't working or if it had just run out of charge. I looked at it dumbly, as if I could bring it to life by sheer willpower. And then I threw it on my bed, picked up the candle, stomped out of the room and headed back out to the veranda.

I took my usual seat on the old couch and once again looked out at the vast spread of dark bush and the rolling grassland that shimmered in the moonlight.

I tried to think about what Will had said. He was right – even if something had gone wrong, there was nothing I could really do about it until morning. I didn't fancy taking a night-time walk to our nearest neighbour, especially seeing as they were almost forty-five minutes away, and I really didn't fancy riding my pushie into town. Not in the dark on our bumpy dirt road, no way. If I didn't stack going over a pothole or corrugation then I'd surely hit an unseen roo that had decided then and there was a great time to bound in front of me. I don't know how the old man managed to drive home drunk.

And so I just looked at the great patch of darkness where the crazy swirl of bright colour given off by the party had been.

More muffled words rode on the wind, the cries of the party-people once again reduced to faintly whispered and rather bizarre non-sequitors. It's funny, but I'd expected to see headlights cutting through the darkness. Considering how many people had made their way to the party by car, surely some of them had thought to drive out and see what was what. But even though I was out there a long time, I didn't see a single one.

There was nothing but those random words floating on the slight breeze, the only evidence that the party had ever been there.

"...won't start..."

"Help...

"...just plain dead."

"I charged it this morning, it can't be..."

"...even the solar is out."

"Please, won't someone..."

"...stop, stop doing that."

"Bullshit..."

"...useless, just bloody..."

"Sis, the cars are dead too."

I must have fallen asleep again, because the next thing I remember is Will yelling that at me. No "wakey wakey," or "hey Sis, sorry, but something else is wrong," or anything polite like that, just a loud voice in my ear.

A really loud voice.

"Yeah, good morning, dickhead," I said.

He ignored my insult and got straight to it.

"So, like I said, the cars aren't working."

"I heard you, I heard you. Just give me a sec, alright?"

"Yeah, alright."

"And put some coffee on."

He looked at me and smiled.

"No power, remember?"

"Do you need power to light a fire? I mean, that's why we've got the pot-belly."

"Okay, okay. Jeez..."

He walked away, muttering to himself, snide remarks that were intentionally just loud enough for me to hear. Isn't brotherly love a wonderful thing?

I stretched and yawned, popped my shoulders and cracked my back. Sleeping on the couch always fucked me up a bit. I got to my feet and stretched some more, trying to work the soreness out of my body. I looked at the party site. Even though it was only early, some people had already left on foot. Their paths across the rolling grassland in the distance were just faint black lines, the people themselves rendered tiny and insignificant in comparison to the land.

They were like columns of ants crossing a dirt road...

I headed inside and went to the toilet, and then stopped in the kitchen and drank some water. Will had had some success with the fire – the smell of coffee was starting to fill the house. I dropped my empty glass in the sink and then joined him by the pot-belly stove. He was already spooning sugar into my cup, and I almost snatched it off him.

"Thanks, bro."

"Yeah, no worries."

I took a sip, burning my tongue. I blew on the coffee, cooling it down, and then took another sip, and then another and then another.

I slowly started to wake up.

"What's the plan?" I asked, breaking the silence.

Will was always an early bird; I wasn't surprised that he'd checked the cars while I'd been snoozing away, so I figured that he'd already worked out what to do next.

"I'll probably ride over to the Johnson's place and see if they know anything. If they aren't home, then I'll head into town, maybe see if I can find the old man."

"Right-oh."

"How about you?"

"I guess I'll knock off my chores, and check on the stock and let them out and all that. But I don't know how I'll feed them if the ute's dead. "

"You'll figure something out. Or you could just walk them down to the bottom paddock, it's still pretty grassy there."

"Good one."

"You could disconnect the water pump too, so we can use the taps on the tanks once we've drained the pipes."

"Okay."

I was still pretty sleepy, and monosyllables were all I could manage.

"I'll leave you to it, then."

"Good luck out there."

"You bet, see you in a few..."

He stomped out of the kitchen – he used to stomp everywhere – and I watched through the window as he strapped on his helmet, hopped on his bike and rode off, a tiny cloud of dust billowing behind him.

I finished my coffee, ate a couple of slices of bread with vegemite, made a second coffee and then headed back out to the veranda. The world was quiet and calm, but the party site was busy with movement, busier than it had been earlier, teeming with people bustling about and rushing back and forth.

I sipped at my coffee and watched them bustle and rush.

As confused as they may have been, at least they didn't have to spend the day working on a farm that had suddenly become a nineteenth-century version of itself. I groaned aloud, knowing that chores and jobs that were already boring and taxing were about to grow even more mind-numbing and back-breaking.

But still, once I'd finished my coffee I got to it.

I CAME BACK FROM FIXING a hole in the rabbit-proof fence to find Will and three party-people arguing outside the house. Will still had his helmet on; I assumed that he'd turned up to find them waiting on our doorstep. And there was still no sign of the old man. I was grateful for that – he hated "their type," and there's nothing like the threat of violence to ruin your day.

"Mate, I'm not asking for much," said one of the party-people, a tall guy with a great pile of dreadlocks wound into a bunch on top of his head.

They must have been so heavy and hot...

"All we need is a little help," another of the party-people said, a short and stocky girl with about a million piercings.

"Yeah, man," said another.

His eyes were glazed and he sounded very far away and he occasionally twitched and sometimes hugged himself and shivered, despite the heat. I figured that he was just another space cadet, and that he probably thought this was all a drug-heightened adventure rather than a half-baked standoff.

"Why should I help you freaks?" Will asked, almost shouting the words. "What have you ever done for us?"

I looked on in disbelief.

"William!" I yelled. "Cut it out."

"But..."

"Don't give me that. What's with you, bro? Look at them. They need help, for fuck's sake. Why can't you hear them out?"

"But..."

"Just shut it, alright?"

He deflated, all his bluster draining away. I turned to the party-people and looked them up and down. I didn't recognise them, but I tried to smile warmly.

"G'day. Are you guys okay?"

"Yeah, we've lost power down at the party," the short and stocky girl said. "Hell, someone with an old ham radio couldn't even get a signal from overseas. And the cars are dead, too. "

"Same here, it's weird. So, what's up?"

"It's our friend back at camp," the girl continued. "She's got asthma and she's lost her puffer. With all the dust everyone's kicking up, she's, you know, she's having a hard time. And with the cars out of action, well..."

I looked over at Will. He'd had asthma as a kid but he'd grown out of it, and he really was feeling for them, a sudden look of concern on his face.

"I get it, I get it," I said, looking back at the girl. "You've probably passed this place dozens of times, we're your nearest neighbour after all. But, sorry, none of us have asthma. Well, not anymore."

"Oh," the girl said, her half-smile collapsing.

"The Alexander's youngest daughter has got it, though," I said, pointing to a house halfway across the valley.

I knew it was there, but I guess all they could see was a speck.

"Far-out," the space cadet said.

He looked at me, his eyes so puffy and hooded that I was surprised he could see anything at all.

And then he winked.

"Knock it off, you idiot," the girl said to him.

"Alright, alright," he said, his voice sulky and whiney.

And then he looked at me again.

"Got a toilet?" he asked. "I need to take a piss."

I sighed, and then pointed to a row of trees at the edge of the house block, just next to the old man's shed. I watched him stagger away, and then turned back to the other two party-people.

"Look, come inside and I'll draw a map," I said.

I turned and they started following, when Will grabbed my arm.

"Sis, I need to talk to you about what I saw in town," he said.

"That can wait, bro. This is more important."

"But..."

"We'll talk about it later, alright?"

I shook him off and walked inside. Will and the two party-people sat at the dining table, while I hunted around for some paper and a pen. Will didn't speak to them while they tried to make small talk, and the atmosphere was suddenly horribly awkward.

I finally found what I was looking for.

I sat down next to the party-people and quickly drew a rough map and talked them through it. I offered them some water, and they topped up their bottles. I offered them a cuppa, but they declined.

"We'd better get a move on," the girl said. "Our mate's pretty sick."

"Fair enough."

Suddenly, the front door slammed open and the space cadet strode in carrying the old man's shotgun. I froze, and somewhat stupidly wondered where he'd found it. I guess the old man had once again forgotten to lock the gun-safe out in the shed after going out spotlighting with his barfly mates.

But there it was and there the space cadet stood.

He was still swaying a little and looked lost behind his eyes, but he had a firm grip on the shotgun.

"Look what I found," he said.

He held the gun up, striking a pose. I quickly got to my feet, and Will and other two party-people followed. We stood there in a bunch, watching the space cadet in confusion and fear. He smiled slyly, and then held the shotgun properly and took aim. I hoped to Christ that the old man hadn't left it loaded – if the space cadet even twitched, he'd hit us all for sure. Out of the corner of my eye, I saw Will tense up, and the other two party-people freeze, overcome with fear and not knowing what to do.

"Bang," the space cadet said.

And that's when Will jumped in front of us.

ABOUT THE AUTHOR

Lachlan Walter is a writer, science-fiction critic and nursery-hand (the garden kind, not the baby kind). He is the author of two books: the deeply Australian post-apocalyptic tale The Rain Never Came, and the upcoming Kaiju story-cycle We Call It Monster. He also writes science fiction criticism for Aurealis magazine and reviews for the independent 'weird music' website Cyclic Defrost, his short fiction can be found floating around online, and he has completed a PhD that critically and creatively explored the relationship between Australian post-apocalyptic fiction and Australian notions of national identity. He loves all things music-related, the Australian environment, overlooked genres and playing in the garden, and he hopes that you're having a nice day. For more information, check out www.lachlanwalter.com

A Spark of Youth

Marcus Turner

JEEZ, WATCH IT, GRANDMA!

Dahlia turned her head, braking the scooter sharply. She glowered at the teenage boys as they swaggered up the ramp three-abreast, laughing. Had her voice not crackled like cellophane when she spoke these days, betraying frailty rather than wrath, she would have given them quite the tongue-thrashing. Her blistering look would have to suffice.

There was a time when men would have made way for a lady, especially one nearing the end of her long march. Now weak, manicured ruffians wrapped in thousand-dollar suits, stiff with self-importance, shoved ahead of her in supermarket queues and looked the other way while she struggled by with her groceries on the short but difficult journey home. Getting her groceries home was much easier, now that she'd swallowed her pride and bought one of these beastly scooters, but the young continually found new ways to insult her. She vowed next time to simply run them down if they were too rude to move. Her Hubert would never have treated her that way, nor any other woman for that matter. Mothers just didn't make them like they used to.

Dahlia continued down the ramp, past the lower-level carpark towards the street. Somewhere inside she heard a car's engine revving loudly, and the screech of tyres. *Idiots. Idiots and ingrates everywhere.* She sped up. She just wanted to get home, away from the unpleasantness of this new and savage world.

The scooter surged across the long pedestrian crossing dividing the ramp in two. Dahlia was halfway across when the loud, screeching vehicle—a towering silver four-wheel drive—tore around the corner, barely missing the pillar closest to Dahlia's side of the crossing. By then it was too late. Life didn't flash before her eyes—only the headlights did, accompanied by the angry bleating of the horn. It was coming too fast, there was no way to—

HEAVEN WASN'T BEAUTIFUL. It was dark, flashing intermittently with harsh fluorescent light—a freeway tunnel hurtling towards a fathomless precipice. Angels flitted above her: angels with horribly smooth faces; mouthless, with only the suggestion of noses, and eyes flaring like St Elmo's Fire on molten quicksilver. The universe spun on its axis, too drunk for terror.

"We're losing her."

I'm not lost, she thought, her mind teetering on the edge of the thoughtless, mindless abyss. *I'm right where I should be. Waiting for my Father to answer the door. Knocking on Heaven's door.* Where had she heard that before? Somewhere, now too far away to remember...

"She's slipping; she's going into cardiac—!"

Emma, she tried to whisper, though she could hear nothing over the sudden hiss.

The angels swarmed above her, and though the title of the song slipped by, the melody overwhelmed her thoughts—the last spark of dying neurons—drowning out the angels' muttering. She floated on the ghostly vibrations over a gleaming sea before slipping below the black waters. It was a good song to go out on.

IF DEATH WAS A SLEEP, then it was fully without dreams. Light sliced through the weave of oblivion, and its return only made oblivion's dreamless and utter finality that much more final, bringing back that frantic scrabbling for the known, the most primal of human terrors fully realised by their sheer absence.

Dahlia Vera Chapman surfaced, eyes flickering, her tired heart quickening with fright.

The room materialised as the brightness slowly receded, bringing back familiar edges and surfaces: she was lying in a bed with coarse sheets, the astringent smell of disinfectant prickling her nostrils. The steady beep of a heart monitor; the susurrus of endless human traffic outside the door; a commanding female voice speaking over the PA system.

A hospital? Then in a flash, she saw the four-wheel drive barrelling down on her scooter, and she reached up to touch a sudden pain in her brow.

The door handle turned with a soft click and a doctor—early forties, dark thinning hair—entered the room. He started with surprise when he noticed Dahlia watching him, giving away both his unpreparedness and the prognosis.

"Gosh," he said, clapping his chest with a nervous laugh. "You scared the daylights out of me." Then he smiled, reassuming his professional dignity. "You're awake."

Dahlia struggled to form words around quivering, incoherent thoughts. "How ... long?" she finally managed, her voice crackling from disuse.

The doctor—*Dr Joseph Cumberbatch,* his name-tag read—consulted the clipboard at the end of the bed. "Three weeks and two days. Not long after surgery, you fell into a coma. Probably best, under the circumstances."

Dahlia looked at him questioningly, grappling in silence and frustration for words. "You died three times on the operating table," he explained. "Each time we didn't think we'd be able to revive you, but you keep clawing your way back." Dr Cumberbatch flashed her an admiring smile. "If you don't mind me speaking frankly, you're one tough old bat. You've got the spark of youth in you."

He removed a thin flashlight from his pocket, clicked it on, and shone it in her eyes. The brightness—the freeway tunnel all over again—burned in each eye, and she blinked to block it out. "How are you feeling? Can you talk? Can you tell me your name?"

"Dh–Dah–*Dahlia,*" she croaked.

"Good. Do you remember what happened?"

The lights flashed, and the horn blared, the engine roaring like a demon—

"C-car," she whispered.

"Good," Dr Cumberbatch said. "Don't worry now, Mrs Chapman, just take it easy for now. Your daughter's been at your bedside the entire time. She must have just gone out for coffee."

"Emma?"

"Good," the doctor remarked. "It's good to see your memory still seems intact. There're no obvious signs of brain damage, which is what we were worried about for a patient of your age, but we'll have a better idea after some further testing. If this is any indication, I think your faculties might be almost good as new."

A patient of your age. The thought came unbidden and fully formed in its bitterness. As the doctor slid the flashlight back into his breast pocket, preparing to leave, Dahlia rasped, quite clearly: *"It's rude to keep mentioning a woman's age, don't you know that?"*

Dr Cumberbatch looked back, surprised once more, noting the lack of strain that had been evident on her face during her previous attempts to speak. He offered her an apologetic smile. "Mrs Chapman, I have a feeling you'll outlive us all."

DAHLIA SPENT ANOTHER two weeks in the hospital, and Emma came by regularly with flowers and hugs. The cloud on Emma's face lifted as the outlook grew brighter. Dr Cumberbatch—along with a string of neurosurgeons and other specialists—were baffled and amazed by Dahlia's rapid recovery. "We've never seen anything quite like it," Dr Cumberbatch told Emma. "A woman her age, it just does not seem possible that she could regain all her faculties so quickly—"

"I can still hear you, you know," Dahlia accosted him, but smiled, having decided that Dr Cumberbatch and his fellows did not mean it any other way than complimentary.

"Does that mean she'll be able to leave soon?" Emma asked.

"I'd like to run some final scans and tests, but assuming she clears them, as I'm expecting—then yes, you'll be able to take her home."

Emma smiled, and palpable relief broke on her face. She'd been away from Paul and the kids for so long, Dahlia thought guiltily. Paul had to work extra hours to keep them afloat; Emma had exhausted all of her paid leave. Poor Myra and Ben must be missing both their parents like crazy.

"*But* given the you-know-what factor," Dr Cumberbatch said in a low voice, "I don't think it's a good idea that she stays alone. This probably isn't the thing you want to discuss right now, but with what she's been through, and you living so far away, it's important to start thinking about her living options."

Emma nodded, her face crumpling. "Yes, I know. I'll stay with her for a little longer while we sort that out."

Dahlia rolled onto her side, facing away, guilt almost too heavy for her old bones to carry.

"EMMA, GO HOME, I'LL be fine," Dahlia told her daughter, as she reached into the wardrobe and pulled out a blouse, laying it on the bed.

"No, you're not fine. You've just had a horrific accident and you need to take it easy. Here, let me help you." Her voice was terse, edging on open frustration.

"I told you, I feel fine." And it wasn't a lie—she hadn't felt this good in years. Even that final week in the hospital, she'd felt good, even spry. Dr Cumberbatch and his staff had been flummoxed not just by the return of her faculties, but the *improvement* of them. "I've put you out enough. Paul and the children need you more than I do."

"Mum, I'm not leaving you", she said, helping Dahlia remove the hospital nightie. "Paul and I are going to dis— Huh."

Dahlia crossed her arms over her naked breasts, shrinking from Emma's scrutiny. "What?"

"You look ... different."

Dahlia snatched her bra from the doona, scowling. "Don't stand there gawking at your poor mother. Help me put this on."

WHEN SHE WAS CERTAIN Emma was asleep, Dahlia climbed out of bed and crept to the bathroom. Emma was a constant shadow, fretting and fussing over her—not that she didn't appreciate it— but her worrying was etching premature lines on her lovely face. And she wasn't being coy when she kept waving Emma away: her bones didn't groan or ache the way they had done the past couple of years; she wasn't reduced to a sluggish crawl or holding the wall as she moved down the hallway anymore; and most tellingly, *she could hold her bladder again.* Even her mind felt sharper, her memories clearer—but with them a different sort of pain. She found herself missing Hubert more in the past fortnight than she had since his passing twelve years ago.

She relieved herself and, as she washed her hands, became transfixed by her face in the mirror. Emma was right: she was looking different. Her face looked plumper, less drawn, as if the sags around her cheeks and neck had ... receded somehow. Even some of the dark spots around her forehead seemed smaller. She looked less like the seventy-nine-year-old she was and more like she had during her fifties.

Dahlia shook her head. *No, it's your imagination. Maybe there was some brain damage after all.* She realised the water was still running so she reached down to turn off the tap when she stopped and stared at her hand. *No ... not possible.* She'd had a liver spot the size of a five-cent coin on the back of her right hand, just below the wrist, for the better part of a decade—too much sun in her youth; she'd even had it checked to make sure it wasn't cancerous. She couldn't remember the last time she'd really noticed it—only that it had been there when waking up in the hospital—*but it wasn't there now. This is too crazy,* she thought, staring at her reflection, caught in a riptide of commingled admiration and horror. *It can't be real...*

She hurried out of the bathroom, into the lounge room and started pulling photo albums out of the wicker basket she had beside the old turntable. She flicked through the pages, scanning furiously, because that face in the mirror... It was cut straight out of a picture from twenty-five years ago. She could see it in her mind's eye, clear as a high-spring afternoon.

Dahlia rifled through three more albums until she found the photograph she was looking for: a faded close-up of herself standing by the old orange tree, wearing a pink-flowered sun-dress, smiling broadly, hair the colour of iron. She took it back to the bathroom, holding it alongside her reflection, eyes moving between the two images. She forced a smile to match the photo. The lines around her mouth and brow; the weight of time finally beginning to tug at her neck, slowly but surely—the two women were identical. The only difference was the hair colour.

No, wait … Dahlia's jaw slowly fell open as she watched dark grey slice up from the roots of each individual hair, moving upwards from the middle of her hairline like a Roman spear, streaking and plumping the thin, cotton-like white threads.

This is impossible, Dahlia thought, before the image of the flashing and honking four-wheel drive roared into her head. *I'm seeing things … The doctors said there was no brain damage, but they missed it. I'm … I'm losing my marbles.*

She dropped the photo next to the sink and scuttled back to her bedroom, but her eyes refused to shut. She laid awake until dawn peered under the curtains.

EMMA OPENED THE DOOR and knocked lightly. "Mum? You awake?"

Dahlia croaked yes, hidden beneath the doona.

"How are you feeling? You want a tea or something?"

"Coffee."

"Coffee?" Emma asked with a frown. "You sure that's a good idea?"

"Believe me, tea's not going to cut it this morning."

Emma took a step into the room. "Mum ... Are you feeling okay?"

"I'm fine, I ... I just didn't sleep well."

"Well, this is why the doctor prescribed you the painkillers, but you refused to put in the script. Anyway, I'll go get your tea."

"Coffee."

"Right. Listen, Mum. I need to go out for a little bit today, sort a few things out. Will you be okay on your own for a few hours?"

"Yes, sweetie."

"Sure?"

"Positive."

"Okay. I'll be back in a few minutes."

Emma returned with the cup and saucer and put them on the bedside table, then sat down on the bed. "I found this in the bathroom. It's one of your old photos from our old place. Dunno how it got there."

Dahlia silently cursed. In her alarm she'd forgotten to put it away.

"Mum," Emma started. "Can you come out and look at me? We need to talk. Please?"

Dahlia didn't move.

Emma sighed. "I— We need to figure out what we're going to do with you. I can't leave you here by yourself, but I don't know how we're going to manage—"

"You don't need to worry about me," Dahlia said. "I'll be okay on my own, I have been for the past twelve years."

"But you *can't* stay on your own!" Emma snapped. "This is really hard on me, you know. I won't let you keep living alone, but with my mortgage, the kids' tuition fees and everything else, Paul and I are struggling. I need to find a solution we can afford that'll guarantee you're being cared for. But I need you to stop being so stubborn and fighting me on this."

Dahlia squeezed her eyes shut. Hot tears scoured her cheeks.

"*Will you get out from under that blanket and look at me!*"

"Emma. I can't."

"Why the hell not?"

"Even if I showed you, you wouldn't believe it."

"Can you stop with the bullshit—" Emma growled, pulling the doona away, and stopped in her tracks. Her face dropped, expressionless. Tears glimmered in the morning sunlight on frozen cheeks. "*Mum*... What happened to you? You're..."

"So it's not a figment of my imagination," Dahlia said, looking down.

"What— How is this possible?"

"I don't know. Ever since the accident, I feel like something's been changing inside me. First it was just things like my memory and arthritis. Then last night ... I saw myself *change* in the mirror, right before my eyes. Like magic."

Emma's eyes bulged with incredulity. "Yeah, but ... that's impossible. I mean—"

"It doesn't make a lick of sense, I know," Dahlia said. "But at least now I know I'm not crazy."

"I'm starting to think *I* am, though. But Mum... this is fantastic." A smile crept its way across Emma's lips. "I mean, you're *reverse-aging*. Never mind how impossible that sounds. Look at you! You look fantastic! This is a new beginning for you!" She laughed. "The doctors are going to go crazy when—"

"No! Nobody's going to know, especially the doctors. At best they'll treat me like a lab rat, a scientific curiosity, and at worst, a circus freak."

"But what about your friends? What about Paul and the kids? How—?"

"Strange thing is," Dahlia replied, "I think I can control it, sort of. Last night when I was in front of the mirror, I used that photo you found to compare. Up to that point everything but my hair had changed. When I stared at the photo, my hair began to change to the same grey it was years ago. Maybe I can change it both ways."

Emma stood up, determination wrought in her expression. "I think we might need to run a couple of tests."

She left the room swiftly, almost running. She returned a few minutes later with two photographs and handed them to Dahlia. One was a picture of herself at Christmas three years ago, age seventy-six; the other was a Polaroid, more faded than last night's picture and more worn around the edges. It was the summer she'd met Hubert: they'd spent the day at the beach, soaking in the sun and splashing flirtatiously in the sea; then afterwards they'd attended a moonlight dance under the stars, colourful bulbs wrapped around the balcony poles and eaves. Hubert's hand rested above her hip as they danced, his other hand entwined in hers. Gosh, he was handsome. Her hair was jet black and wavy like the ocean they'd swam in, her skin flawless and creamy. She was twenty-two in that picture.

"Try that one first," Emma said.

Dahlia frowned in concentration, fixing her gaze on the Polaroid in her hand. She did that for perhaps thirty seconds, shaking with effort.

"It's not working," Emma said, disappointed.

"Let me try something." Dahlia got up and headed towards the bathroom, Emma following behind her.

Dahlia held the Polaroid up next to the mirror and focused her gaze upon her two selves; she shut out Emma's intrusion and concentrated. Her eyes slowly shifted between the two, circling in a lazy figure-eight.

Suddenly, Emma raised a hand to her mouth. "Oh my God."

EMMA SMILED AND ROSE from the bench when she spotted Dahlia moving up the path towards her. They embraced, mist from the fountain gently dappling their wrinkled skin. The sun was high and the sky was clear, but the warmth had long since ebbed from the days. The trees in the park were mostly bare, their leaves long since migrated to populate the ground, and there was an unmistakable chill in the air. It would soon be too cold for two little old ladies to stroll among the trees.

"You're looking good, Emma."

"So are you," Emma smiled. "But you can put your young suit on. I don't mind."

Dahlia smiled sheepishly and glanced around, trying not to look relieved. Being a Tuesday morning and a bit too chilly for anyone other than inner-city joggers, the park was empty. She closed her eyes and concentrated on her twenty-year-old self. She hardly felt the transformation anymore; it usually took less than a minute these days. Still risky, out here in the open, but she'd gotten so used to living in her younger form—and the perks of youth—that it was worth saving the battle against fatigue and keeping in the warmth for another day.

"Wow," Emma said. "You're getting so good at controlling it."

Dahlia smiled, her eyes following the path, but said nothing.

"I know why you do it. The old suit, I mean. It has its uses, but on days like today, you don't have to hide yourself for my benefit. It's not your fault. You shouldn't feel guilty for something you had no control over."

Dahlia sighed. "I know. But you'll never know what it's like to watch your only child become an old lady while you stay the same age forever, if you want to."

"I might be getting on in years, Mum, but I'm not licked yet," Emma replied with a wink, flashing a sickle of yellowing teeth.

"Sorry, I didn't mean to—"

"It's okay."

They meandered for a moment in reflective silence.

"Do you think you'll die someday, too?" Emma asked.

Dahlia remembered nothing of her three times dancing the *danse macabre* some twenty years ago, except a vague sense of some bluesy rock song playing, and the certainty that nothing waited for her on the other side. *We cling to life so desperately,* she mused, *for fear of it being taken away; but when you realise the absolute nothingness on the other side, the complete cessation of anything conscious, and suddenly have it reinstated—well ... you become greedy, guarding the prize of youth jealously.*

So few people realise what treasures they have in ignorance, the fleetingness of memory, the temporariness of life; how some pains and losses fade with those autumn years.

"Mum?"

"Sorry. Wool-gathering."

"Still an old lady at heart, huh?"

"Mmm."

"So?"

Dahlia took a deep breath. "I don't know if I can die."

"You ... couldn't control it if you wanted to? Just set the clock forward and wait out the final minutes."

"I don't think it works that way."

"Forever young."

"It's not as great as it sounds," Dahlia told her. *It's a curse, watching everything you love fade away while the memories become clearer and sharper like a knife. A knife that will pierce my heart but never kill me. Knowing something you created from love will wink out into nothingness while you linger, despairing for the memory.*

"How are the kids?" Dahlia asked, suddenly changing the subject.

"They're getting by. Ben's little one is growing up too fast, and his job keeps him busy. Myra and her husband are struggling a bit, though—don't know the full story, but I think he might have been sleeping around. While she's pregnant with his second child, no less. They're both missing their father a lot right now."

"I bet. Paul was a good man."

"How's the dating going for you, Mum?"

Dahlia flapped a hand in disdain. "Oh, I can't relate to today's men. They're all so prickly or self-absorbed. Nothing like your father."

"He was one of a kind."

"One in a lifetime," Dahlia said, needles pricking inside her chest.

"I think you should keep trying. Lots of fish in the sea. This has been a new beginning for you; that we should all be so lucky. We all need company when the road is so long. Heck, you deserve it."

Company, Dahlia thought, *on a trek that might never end; another person I'll love that I'll have to watch die.*

"I'm glad I had you on this journey with me," Dahlia said.

Emma reached out with a liver-spotted hand and squeezed Dahlia's. "Hey, you've still got me. For as long as it can last."

Dahlia closed her eyes, blinking away tears. As much pain as this moment would bring, one day far from now, she squeezed back tighter, greedily holding onto that love and happiness like she could make them last forever.

About the author

Marcus Turner spent most of his childhood in Bega, NSW, before moving around between Sydney, Broken Hill, Brisbane, and finally settling in Melbourne in 2005, where he now lives with his wife and two children. He is currently studying a Bachelor of Arts with a Professional Writing and Publishing major at Curtin University, and runs a beauty-supply business with his wife. He is presently in the final stages of a novella, A Rose for the Damned, and is also working on his first novel, Land of the Righteous. A Spark of Youth is his first published work. He writes mostly within the speculative fiction genre, predominantly leaning towards horror

and sci-fi elements.

In his spare time, Marcus is a hardcore gamer, metalhead, and horror film/literature aficionado, particularly fond of the works of H.P. Lovecraft. If the apocalypse comes because dead-and-dreaming Cthulhu has finally woken up, chances are Marcus had a hand in it. He is also apparently prone to delusions of nightmarish (and short-sighted) grandeur.

You can find and connect with him on:
Facebook: https://www.facebook.com/MarcusTurnerWriter
Instagram: @marcusturnerwriter
Website: streamofmadness.wordpress.com (COMING SOON)

The Washer Woman's Favourite

Maureen Flynn

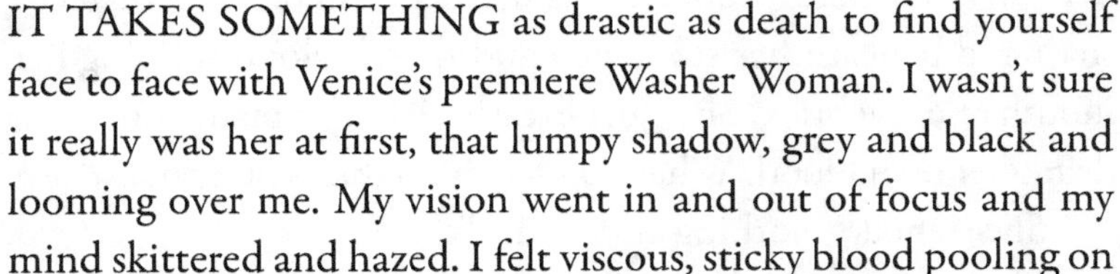

IT TAKES SOMETHING as drastic as death to find yourself face to face with Venice's premiere Washer Woman. I wasn't sure it really was her at first, that lumpy shadow, grey and black and looming over me. My vision went in and out of focus and my mind skittered and hazed. I felt viscous, sticky blood pooling on my right side where I'd stabbed the knife in deep.

"Now dearie," she crooned. "Why don't you tell me what I have here?"

Before I could even process her words, she was kneeling beside me, a wad of shapeless fabric in her hand, now pressed tight against my injured side.

"I'm buying you an extra ten," she said, sucking thoughtfully at the side of her mouth. "So get talking before I regret saving you from my poor, hungry rats."

My grandmum had told me about the rats. The woman mentioning them was the first hint that I'd found the real Washer Woman after all.

My tongue felt thick, too big for my mouth. Pain arced through me and I felt cold and sick. Still, I could hear Alina gasping behind the Washer Woman, choking on bubbling blood. It was now or never. I had to make the Washer Woman understand.

The Washer Woman must have seen the panic in my eyes because she lent in close until I could smell her breath and said, "Ah. That old chestnut, is it? Venice's answer to Romeo and Juliet."

She bent in even closer, so that her eyes drilled down into mine. "She's still alive. Just." My heart fluttered with hope.

"Not for much longer though," she added. "They've broken her jaw good and proper on that brick. There's bits of teeth shattered beneath her stone bed and there's blood staining her mouth and the brick. She can't breathe. They've made sure she'll drink her own blood. What do you say to that, young man?"

She sighed. "Nothing at this rate."

Placing a long, gnarled finger on my forehead, a charge of something bolted through me and she tilted her head. "Better?"

Any remaining doubts I had that she was The Washer Woman vanished like fog in a wind. The half here, half there sensations faded into background noise. My vision felt clearer and my tongue could move off the roof of my mouth.

"Help," I managed in a whisper. "A ... A ... Alina."

"Yes, yes." The Washer Woman grinned; all teeth and danger and devoid of empathy. Just like in Grandmum's stories. "I don't have all day. I have precious clothes to wash and less precious spirits to eat. Slowly. Like the chit behind me."

I could see her clearer now that she'd worked her magic on me. Her face was wizened and small and her wrinkled skin hung in folds. She was the oldest of the ancients. Her nose was button-like, just as Grandmum used to say, to fool the innocents into thinking The Washer Woman could be kind. *That's why the bright coloured dresses too*, Grandmum had told me. *Tied up in different directions to keep clean as she traverses Venice's wet depths in a riot of parrot brightness. But then you see her eyes, deep and black and full of malice, and that's when you know you've found trouble. She got no choice about being the Goddess of Washing so she takes it out on the rest of us.*

Remembering Grandmum gave me pause. She'd rouse on me if she saw my designs now. But then I closed my eyes, remembered Alina and her perfect white skin, sea witch eyes and copper hair and knew I couldn't consign her to this fate.

"You've gone silent again, boy," The Washer Woman said, "and this time being close to death is no excuse. Save Alina, you say, and why should I? She's been marked as mine with that brick and you know it. The Doge knows to keep me content down here. Haven't you heard the stories too, idiot child? No one wants me left hungry. Who's to say I won't come up into the light and really start feeding."

"Of course I know," I managed in short bursts. "Why else do you think I stabbed myself over her body?" The Washer Woman's eyes widened. Something beyond rage and fury surfaced in her eyes—curiosity.

"Do you have a proposal for me?" Her messily made up lips pursed with interest.

"Feed off me instead," I said. "I'd last longer. Sacrificial love always does, doesn't it?"

"You'd let me crush your mouth with the brick and take you? No one has ever asked such a thing before."

"Perhaps they've never loved as hard as I have."

"In all of Venetian history? You jest."

I groaned. It didn't matter. Time slipped away while we talked.

"Do you accept my offer or not?"

Something in her face softened. Was it pity and kindness I could sense? Surely not.

"It's a high price you'd be paying, love. You'd want to be damned sure your sacrifice was worth it."

"Make it happen," I said through gritted teeth. "Get it over with."

The Washer Woman didn't hesitate a second time. She moved out of my vision and I winced when she pulled the brick none too gently out of Alina's mouth. I couldn't hear sounds from Alina any more. My love was slipping away.

And then I could focus on nothing but the excruciating pain in my mouth as well as in my side as The Washer Woman wrenched my head back and pushed hard till my teeth shattered.

GRANDMUM SAT CROUCHED on her low wooden stool, leaning forward as she beat fabrics against the side of a big wooden bucket. I loved her scent of soap and pomander even then—somehow both comforting and exotic. I sat at her feet, neatening the dirt by raking my nails through it.

"Do you know the secret of Venice?" she rapped out suddenly, like a teacher starting a lesson.

"Yes. It floats on wood like magic."

Grandmum cackled. "And that's not all it floats on, lovely. Many years I've sat here pounding and washing rich folk's dresses—I've seen it all. Sin and hatred and pestilential hunger, housing the flesh of the dead and their wandering spirits below. And Venice's own Goddess of Darkness? She found an affinity with me. She'll not touch me or mine as long as we keep our wits about us."

I shrank back at her fey laughter.

"Mara, my ninny daughter, she won't tell you the truth, no. And no one else in this town will tell you either. Too terrified of she that marks this place with her rage, and they, they begged for it."

"What did they beg for, Grandmum, and who's she, who's this Goddess of Darkness?" I asked wide-eyed.

"You want to know do you, boy? You want to know the real secret of this City of Water?"

She stretched her wrinkled hand out, curled her gnarled fingers into my hair tightly.

"It's a city of masks above and below, child. And a city of underground, masticating spirits beneath a city of rising waters. I'd know. I wash for a living. She keeps away from me out of respect, because I know tough stains when I see them."

"Who?" I croaked, shivers travelling up and down my spine. "Who do you mean?"

"Bettista," Grandmum snapped. "And don't you forget her, not The Washer Woman. You could call her the original and the best. Venice prayed for its own Goddess and the strength of belief was so great Bettista was formed. Only we didn't pay much attention to how we wanted our Goddess to turn out, did we? Turns out Bettista didn't much like being summoned into existence merely to wash clothes and grant wishes for all eternity just because Venice is wet, so she turned herself terrible and revealed an alarming ability to eat people's souls. Venice has never been the same since."

"NOW THAT'S INTERESTING," The Washer Woman said, sitting back on her haunches. "I thought you had the look of her line. I'm sorry, in my own way, that the girl's lover had to be you, poor Celie's grandson, but then, fate is a strange beast."

I couldn't reply. My head ached and my eyes watered. My mouth felt like a thousand bees stung at once from the inside. And still, I couldn't breathe for the brick in my mouth.

"That was rude of me." The Washer Woman said apologetically. "Feeding off your first memory before I've taken you properly for my own." She rolled up her long, colourful sleeves. "Now to remedy."

Reaching behind her, she pulled out a blue, silk dress, dangling it in front of me. Alina's death shroud. Slowly, The Washer Woman draped the dress over the lower half of my body.

"The Doge knows that when he sends his noble down every ten years, he's got to dress him or her in something full of their memories. Something they've owned a good long time. Helps me to drag the feed out longer. Your lass must have owned this dress awhile. It didn't reach her ankles."

I couldn't speak, but The Washer Woman didn't seem to care. She pushed on.

"You're not dressed in anything special because you aren't the intended sacrifice. But you two were lovers and so this dress surely means something to you. You'll die with your clothing and hers intertwined."

Before I could say a word, she flung up both arms and began to chant.

IN THIS MEMORY, I'M older, yet Grandmum still sits on her little wooden stool washing the rich's clothing, bent backed and her hands stiffer and slower.

On this particular day, she fixed a glare on me. "I've heard you've been eyeing off the Vendramin cousins; Alina and Fiametta. They are vain and selfish and nothing good can come of the likes of us messing with the likes of them."

I scowled, twelve, and full of my own self-importance. Grandmum just laughed. "I was once your age, Diavolo, and I too reached high. I yearned for a Vendramin too. I was courted by Andrea Vendramin for a while, or so I thought, until I was flung out into the mud, the laughing stock of Venice. The embarrassment stung me deep and I have nursed plans of revenge for many a long year."

"You and the Doge of Venice were … " I made kissing noises in the air, too impressed to stay sullen. "Grandmum!"

"And didn't I say it was a mistake," she snapped. "It took me years to find a husband and a trade after that humiliation. I would have thrown myself off the *Ponte di Rialto* if it wasn't for Bettista."

"The Washer Woman," I gasped "You never said…"

"I said she found an affinity with me, nitwit. What did you think I meant?"

My eyes narrowed. "How?"

"She pulled me back from the *Ponte*. Spun me around so fast I didn't know what was happening, and then we were underground, somewhere full of candles and silks fluttering in a soft wind. Someplace beneath."

I whistled, impressed, but Grandmum just laughed.

"I was too dazed to be wowed. Bettista asked me what I was doing. Said that there were enough scum dying every day in this city on top of the Doge's sacrifices to give myself up too. So I told her everything, sobbing all the while. Perhaps she'd grown lonely over the years for I think she felt sorry for me. At any rate, she gave me my Washer Woman trade and wove a spell to ensure that no clothing stains would outdo me and sent me up above. What do you say to that, young man?"

I sucked the side of my mouth thoughtfully. "It's a good story, Grandmum, and you scare me enough that I'd believe it, but I don't understand why I can't have a Vendramin if one of them loves me. I'm not you after all, and Alina is not her uncle."

Grandmum made a face.

WHEN I CAME TO A SECOND time, my whole body tingled, like every nerve was on fire. The ache in my head had become a searing burn and my eyes felt pushed into my face and hollow. I retched, but nothing came up.

"It won't come up, dear. You're dead. A spirit. Incorporeal."

And then The Washer Woman smiled again, that dreadful shark's grin.

"It will hurt more, with each memory I eat, or so the stories go." She sounded sad now. "If you believe them."

"You were friends with Grandmum," I whispered. "Be kind to her grandson."

"Believe me, I was trying to be," she said, full of remorse. "I made the Doge choose in *her* name. I made a promise, after all."

She straightened as my mind reeled in confusion. Before I could untangle what The Washer Woman meant, a hand pushed me backwards.

"Now lie still. I haven't delved into your memories deep enough, and you aren't even crying yet."

THIS TIME, I WALKED through the *Salizzada Cannaregio*. Stall owners beckoned at passersby, selling fresh flowers and spices and silks. In one corner of the path, I could see a mask stall. How intricate the beadwork and how beautiful the overlays of silk are, I thought, and The Doge is hosting a masquerade ball in two days' time. I wanted to buy a mask to gift to Alina, but the cheapest mask would cost me ten years' wages, and I was still young, a mere apprentice in the spice trade.

I turned my gaze back to the water's edge. At any moment, the Vendramin gondola would pass me by, bearing Alina. Smaller, plainer gondolas eased through the water and I admired the way the water sparkled as oars shrove through its depths.

Last night, I had hidden by the Vendramin's big house, waiting for Alina to drop a message from her window. At midnight, she'd dropped a fine lace handkerchief to the ground. I'd picked it up to find lipstick words on its surface.

Cannaregio. Noon.

I knew what Alina meant. The Doge took his daughters and cousins out every day at noon to be admired under his silken umbrellas. Other nobles and the richer merchants would tie their gondolas to the Doge's fine craft and offer expensive drinks and sweets and shower his cousins with compliments in the hopes of a marriage proposal. The Doge's only son had died thanks to the plague. How Grandmum had laughed till she'd choked at that subtle piece of irony. Now he must depend on his nieces and his youngest nephew to rule once he died.

My breath caught as I saw the Doge's gondola pass. Alina was but a small speck in the distance, marked only by her blue silks and flaming hair which glinted in the sunlight. She waved directly at me and blew me a kiss.

WHEN I WOKE UP FOR a third time, my head felt like I'd swallowed too much cold water; aching and freezing and setting my teeth on edge all at once. I felt a tear track down one cheek.

"Was she truly worth it?" The Washer Woman asked with interest. "Did you even get to touch her in the end?"

"I am Celie's grandson, and she meant something to you, so please, be kind." I spoke in shuddering gasps.

"You gave up that right, child. I'm sorry. Celie was my favourite of all the people I've met and I made her a special promise."

And then she touched a hand to my forehead again, and I slumped forward.

SO IT WENT ON. A KALEIDOSCOPE of memories I couldn't halt and all the while more and more pain building inside my head, a pressure valve without release. I relived Alina and I kissing at The Doge's masked ball (she'd stolen me an outfit and a mask both from her brother); flowers dropped at the front of her house and me hiding behind carts and watching as she lifted the flowers to her nose one by one; snatched moments at different city rendezvous points with clumsy kisses on cheeks and mouths; and then, finally, my most precious memory of all.

The *Calle del Perdon*. I'd pressed Alina against a stone wall. No one looked at us twice. It's a poor end of town and Alina wore an old dress I'd 'borrowed' from my mother. Our tongues tangled and Alina's legs wrapped around mine. Her eyes were so green I could have drowned in their enchantment. Sweat poured off both our backs, but we didn't care. We cared about nothing but each other.

In the corner of my memory, an old lady watched us in shadows. Neither of us had seen her then, and even if we had, we wouldn't have cared.

"A MISTAKE, LAD," THE Washer Woman said, as I groaned, full of pain. She looked more solid now, with a healthy gleam in each cheek. Some of her wrinkles had smoothed away and her hair looked grey rather than snow white. "Surely you know who the old lady was?"

I gritted my teeth, shaking my head from side to side. I didn't care for more of The Washer Woman's games. I wanted this over.

"You already know," she said gently, putting a solicitous hand to my forehead. "Look closer."

My eyes closed of their own volition and I saw the scene again from another angle. Long limbed, beautiful Alina pushed against a wall by a strapping, younger version of myself, yes, but an old lady clutching a bundle of clothing and watching with eyes a-glitter with hate from a corner, too. Grandmum.

I felt more than physical pain in my head. This awful ache spread to my chest with thin, pinching fingers. I would have found it hard to breathe if I wasn't already dead.

Grandmum? She had known of Alina and I, yet said nothing?

"Oh-ho, but she didn't say nothing," The Washer Woman cackled. She jabbed a crooked finger into her chest. "She said something to *me*."

And then she knelt down beside me and pressed her lips to my cheeks, one after the other.

GRANDMUM STOOD AT THE *Ponte Di Rialto* in nothing but her night shift. She raised both arms above her head.

"Bettista, Bettista, I have made my choice, and I call in your promise."

The usually still waters of the *Rialto* glittered and lapped against the side of the bridge, then rose in a column of glittering water droplets. Bettista, The Washer Woman, stood on the water column in a dress of greens and blues and browns, her hands clasped together solemnly.

"You called, Celie?"

Grandmum swallowed nervously. "I've waited a long while to call in this favour, but call it in I will. Once, you promised me you'd help me get my revenge on The Doge."

Bettista inclined her head. "Yes, so I did. But you never called. I thought you had forgotten."

Grandmum shook her head. "Not forgotten. Merely waiting for the right moment."

Bettista smiled. "It's such actions as this one which remind me why I liked you. Which of The Doge's relatives have you chosen?"

Grandmum held out a hand to steady herself against the bridge, then adjusted the neck of her dress.

"Alina," she said quietly. "I'll see her in hell."

Bettista laughed. "I must say this is unexpected. I thought you'd choose the little nephew for sure, if only to ruin The Doge's bloodline. Why Alina?"

"Because she is seeing my grandson," Grandmum mumbled, "and I won't have her ruin him the way Andrea ruined me."

"And if they love each other, truly love each other?" Bettista asked with some interest. "What then?"

Grandmum shrugged. "He is a young and foolish boy set to become a merchant and leave this wretched city. He'll find some exotic lass and forget."

Bettista studied Grandmum's face. "So we two must hope." She dismissed her small moment of qualm, if that was what it was, and went on. "It will be done, Celie. I go to see The Doge tonight."

MY EYES WERE GLASSY with shock as I stared at Bettista, The Washer Woman, in horror.

"Yes," The Washer Woman crooned. "It was your own Grandmum who condemned her, and I had to follow through, for a promise is a promise."

I couldn't help it. I imagined the way The Doge must have looked when Bettista had appeared before him in the dead of night, demanding her dues. Too afraid to refuse, Alina's uncle would have stabbed my love himself, and jammed the brick in her mouth hard in his sobbing rage. He had buried her in the family crypt and with each step back towards sunlight, tried to forget. Had he already started to weave new succession plans, thought of ways to push Fiametta forward for a sound marriage, even as careworn lines and a new suffering in his eyes surfaced for the first time? Alina had been the eldest after all, and his favourite.

"Forget him and forget her. Forget them all," The Washer Woman said, drawing herself tall and full of command. "You gave yourself to me in exchange for the girl, and now you are mine. My promises are a double-edged sword. Celie should have been more careful."

I tried to block her cruel words out. I willed myself to my feet, but I was a spirit now, and I floated instead. Bettista, the wretched Washer Woman didn't stop me. Perhaps she was intrigued.

I made myself look down at Alina. Already, her pale skin had a grey tinge and her lips puffed with rot. The Doge had carefully dressed Alina to cover the gash at her neck, but The Washer Woman had removed her dress to drape it over me, so that now the gash sat open to the elements, pink and red and puckered. I reached out spectral fingertips to touch Alina's hair, then her cheeks, then her lips, but my fingers slid right through.

I felt tears rise to choke me. I had exchanged myself for Alina willingly and now Bettista, this realm's underground Queen, had me wound tight. I would spend my days nailed to cold, wet walls. I would spend my night time collared and crawling on my knees. Bettista wouldn't need to compel me to stay. There was no power above or below ground that another could wield to free me. The spell had been cast and all thanks to my own Grandmum!

I couldn't help it. I cried and I cried and I cried at my ill luck. I wished I'd never met Alina, for if I hadn't, she'd still be alive. I cried so hard and so long Venice began to flood. I made sure Grandmum's street flooded first while Bettista looked on, smiling all the while.

About the author

Maureen Flynn lives on the sunny South Coast of NSW with her partner and is an avid speculative fiction and crime lover, writer and fan. Her collection of poetry, My Heart's Choir Sings, a collection about grief, guilt, the blame game and moving on was self-published in 2014 and she religiously reviews Doctor Who on her Inkashlings<https://inkashlings.wordpress.com/> blog. She has finally taken up consultancy in 2018 so she can dedicate more hours of her day to working on novels and short stories. She has two other short story fantasy publications, Gardening through the danse macabe (A hand of knaves, CSFG) and The life and crime of Dr Minnie Isaacs (PhD) (Temporal Fractures, forthcoming Specul8). She also participated in ACT Hardcopy for fiction writers in the 2018 cohort. You can find her on twitter @inkashling

The Beginning of the End

Carolyn Young

OH MY GOD, THE PAIN. Not physical pain; this pain feels like it's ripping my existence apart. Unfamiliar hands, smaller and less hairy than my own, reach out to slam on the emergency brake. Stars appear before me as the thumping of my heart drowns out the high-pitched screech of the brakes. Through blurred vision I look out the windows of the train. The spattering of blood tells me I was too late. No. *He* was too late. This isn't me, my body is lying on the tracks. If this is the beginning of my death, somehow it sucks even more than my life did.

I thought I had it all worked out. Initial pain on impact. Travel towards the light. Flashbacks of my life—not that I was looking forward to that part. My life sucked. Of course it did, otherwise I wouldn't be in this mess. Then nothing. No pain, no regret, no consciousness. Just being absorbed back into the universe. One more piece of cosmic dust.

The last thing I remember is standing on the edge of the platform near the overpass waiting for the express train. Considering the circumstances I'd felt completely calm. This wasn't a spur of the moment impulse which, when acted upon, would be immediately regretted. I'd thought this through planned it—pain, light, sucky flashbacks, nothingness. Something must have gone wrong, terribly wrong. Figures. I can't even do death right. The train driver, whose anguish I feel, loses his lunch as I'm thrown out of his body by his violent heaving.

I stand on the edge of the platform, looking down at my mutilated body with a calm indifference. I'm still not sure what's going on, but while I'm watching the aftermath, I'm joined by an old guy. He's looking at me as he approaches holding his hand out to shake mine.

"I'm Bill. You new here?"

"Mark," I say, shaking his hand firmly.

"Is that you?" he asks, nodding towards the mess covering the tracks.

"Yeah, that's my body. I didn't expect anyone to be able to see me standing here."

"We can all see each other in the beginning. Well those of us who did ourselves in, anyway."

"How long have you been dead?" I ask him.

"A few years now. But don't worry, most don't stay as long as I have," he says, rubbing his fingers over the grey bristles along his jaw line.

"Where do they go?"

"Who knows what's next. I guess we'll both find out soon enough."

"Why are we still here?"

"Maybe we still have something to learn here, and have to stay until we've learned it," he shrugged.

"So how do I know what I have to learn?"

"Don't ask me. It's just a theory, and I obviously don't have the answers. But good luck to you mate, hope you're not trapped here too long."

Turning towards him, I watch him fade away before my eyes. Silly old coot.

I'm guessing this is it. This is death and I'm in hell. I always knew there was a chance that the whole heaven and hell thing actually existed and that when I chose suicide I condemned myself to eternal damnation. Maybe this is it. Closing my eyes I feel a shudder followed by a violent burst of power drawing me away.

I open my eyes when I'm hit by a strong wave of disgust and revulsion. I'm standing holding a pressure hose in one hand and a bucket in the other. But it's not me—I'm in another body. The tracks in front of me are bathed in blood, bone fragments and chunks of flesh. Couldn't the coroner have at least made sure the pieces were gone before they sent in the clean-up crew. This guy's name is Ted and I can hear his thoughts. Right now he's angry. He's going to be having nightmares about this for years. He wishes I'd given some thought to the feelings of those who'd have to clean up this mess before I jumped. He's thinking about the train driver who had to be sedated—poor guy. He sighs and turns on the hose, spraying my remains into the gutter and out of sight.

Another jolt and I'm standing in my sister's hallway as her heart shatters into pieces—the pain, the shock, the regret—I feel it all. Her thoughts are rushed and crazed—if only she'd been a better sister she would have known I needed help. She wishes she'd taken more time out to check on me, but she's been so busy with her husband and kids. The kids—how was she going to explain this to them.

"No Carrie, this wasn't your fault," I try to tell her, but all I feel is the pain and emptiness in her shaking, sobbing body. She can't hear me.

Like ripples in a pond, I'm thrown into different bodies as more people hear of my death. Sometimes I'm thrown out of someone's emotions for a period of time and I can think and feel for myself.

Before my death, I'd been so sure that no one cared about me, but now I feel their powerful emotions as if they were my own. Sadness, grief, emptiness, and regret. It's like living in a washing machine of emotional pain, with little break between cycles. I hadn't realised so many people cared, that my death would impact so many lives. That so many would hurt and feel the loss after I had left this world. But I haven't gone anywhere. Not really. I can feel what they feel, but I can't comfort them. I can't tell them I'm ok where I am. I'm not ok. I just wanted peace. For the pain to go away. But all I feel now is pain, regret and confusion. None of which belong to me—I caused it, but it's not my pain. Will I forever be trapped here by the emotions of those who cared about me? Or is this just the beginning, like Bill said. Will I move on when I've learned what I'm here to learn? There's no way to be sure, but I commit to looking for some kind of sign. I have to try.

The day of my funeral, the chapel is creaking at the seams. All my family are here, my ex-girlfriends, friends and work colleagues. I feel their distress. There's no coffin. There weren't enough pieces of me left to make having one worthwhile. I'm jolted into my mother's thoughts. She's wondering if she did the right thing by not buying a coffin. It seemed a waste to pay for one just to have a focal point for the mourners—maybe it would have been more distressing for them, knowing it was filled with a few bones and a mush of shredded flesh.

I feel her anger. She's mad at me for doing this. Not just to her, but to everyone else in the chapel. She wonders if I have any regrets. I wish I could tell her I've never regretted anything more than I do this, but I can't. Death isn't what I expected and wanted. It's not the peace and nothingness that I craved. I feel Mum's anguish, the jagged, gaping wound in her heart. She thinks she should have known. That looking after me is what a mother is supposed to do. Mothers are supposed to protect their children. She pictures me as a small child, curled on her lap reaching out for her to kiss my pain away. It was her job to look after me, and she feels like she failed. A mother shouldn't have to say goodbye to her son. I reach out to her, trying to tell her it wasn't her fault, but there's no response.

My best mate stands expressionless in the second row, leaning forward to put his hand on my mother's shoulder. At his touch, I'm moved into his perspective. Looking at him you'd think that he felt nothing, but as I'm forced into his consciousness I feel his pain. He's torn up because he didn't go out for a beer with me last time I called. He'd made up some flimsy excuse because he was too tired after work. He'll never forgive himself for not going. Maybe if he'd gone drinking with me he could have saved me—he'd always been good at talking me out of stupid ideas.

I can't even remember how many times he talked me out of driving when I'd had a few too many beers. I wish we'd had that last beer. It wouldn't have changed my mind, but it would have been one last good memory.

My boss is here. He's upset that he kept me back at work the night before I died. Marvin from work is upset that he didn't cover the shift when I'd asked him to. They're thinking that maybe if they'd done things differently I'd still be here.

The next jolt sends me to the train driver. He's sitting at the back of the chapel. His pregnant wife sits beside him as he sobs. I can feel how broken he is, how his thoughts flicker from one thing to another. Why didn't he see me earlier? If only he'd hit the emergency stop button sooner. How is he going to support his wife and baby now that he's too traumatized to work? He keeps seeing images of blood and smashed bones. He hasn't slept properly since it happened. The nightmares keep coming, showing him visions of my detached limbs, forever etched in his mind. He has so many questions, and I can't give him the answers.

When I stood on that platform I didn't think of him, but now I'm filled with overwhelming shame. The strength of my own emotion forces me out of his thoughts and I watch as his body jolts back against the seat. His eyes open wide and the colour drains from his face as his wife tightens her grip around his shoulder.

By the end of my funeral, I feel raw with emotion.

The hardest pain to endure is that of my last girlfriend, Sophie. I loved her so much. As her despair becomes my own I feel her guilt. A feeling of responsibility overwhelms her—it was her fault, she cheated on me. Her stomach sinks again when she pictures my face when I found them in bed together. Why didn't she run after me? Why didn't she tell me it was because she'd got scared by how much she loved me? I work to get the image of her naked body straddling the guy from my mind. His hands were touching her the way mine had that morning. The jealousy grips me like a vice—strong and powerful as I'm thrown out of her thoughts.

THAT NIGHT I'M DRAWN back into in Sophie's emotions. I feel her pain while she sobs, curled up in the bed we used to share. The first time we met begins to play through her mind—I'd offered to buy her a drink, then tripped over my own feet on the way back to give it to her. Our first kiss through her eyes is really something. Did I really look at her that way? My laughter and the goofy movies we watched together wrapped around each other on the couch, runs through her mind. Her sobs become more intense as she remembers the first time we made love. My emotions intertwine with hers as she thinks about the mistake she made that last night. As sick as I feel about it, what she feels is even worse—the self-loathing, guilt and disgust. She'd gone to the pub with friends after work and gotten drunk. She barely remembered meeting him, let alone having sex with him. If I hadn't caught them at it, she probably would have put it down to a bad dream. She feels empty, alone and lost. As my empathy for her overtakes my own feelings of jealousy, I wish I could comfort her, tell her it wasn't her fault, but I can't—I can only remain powerless, constrained within the framework of her pain and distress. I feel it the moment her decision is made—the same relief I'd felt when I decided to step in front of the train. She doesn't want to live with this guilt. She knows it's selfish, but in her despair she can't see any other way to endure the pain.

I'm tempted to let her. If she commits suicide too, she'll be here with me. I can tell her I forgive her, that it wasn't her fault that I died. We can work out this moving on thing together—but what if there is no moving on? I don't want her trapped in this excruciating existence that I'm in—forever trapped in the pain of others.

"No," I scream at her, but she can't hear me. She climbs out of bed and washes the tears from her face. I feel the familiar sense of calm as she considers her options. A train like me? That would be fitting. But she can't get the look on the face of the train driver out of her mind. She can't do that to someone else. A gun? She doesn't have one, or know how to get her hands on one. A knife? She's never been good with blood. She usually faints at the sight of it.

Stumbling into the kitchen, she eyes the knife block sitting on the kitchen benchtop. Pulling each knife out, she runs her finger along the blade. She picks the sharpest one and smiles, running the blade firmly across her wrist. I scream at her to stop. She can't hear me. I can't stop her. The knife isn't sharp enough—it barely breaks the skin. I dare to hope that she'll stop now and go back to bed. She puts the knife back down and looks out the window. The lake. She can't swim. I'm still trapped while she walks out the door, not bothering to stop to put her shoes on, or to close the door behind her.

The night is cold and dark, her feet and heart numb, as she walks down the boardwalk to the pier. She takes one last look back, breathes in and eases herself off the edge and into the dark, freezing water. She pushes firmly against the pier and her body floats into the deeper water. At first I feel her peace, then her panic. She thinks of her parents, her little brother, the kids she wanted to have one day. Her arms and legs thrash around wildly while she decides, then go limp as she accepts her decision—she's ready to die.

"I'm so sorry," she says into the night air.

No, I want to scream, *this isn't the answer.*

"I forgive you," I whisper as her body sinks under the water.

I feel anger and guilt and regret—if I hadn't killed myself she wouldn't be dying right now. This is my fault.

She inhales a huge mouthful of water my consciousness breaks free of hers. I can no longer feel what she's feeling—my own pain overwhelms me once more. I concentrate on all my pain, my guilt and my remorse and push everything towards her. Maybe if I can jolt her, like I did the train driver at the chapel, she might be able to make it to land.

Maybe this will work. I concentrate on my pain and feel my spirit leaving her body. At the last moment, I give her one last hard push. It works. Her body floats towards the edge of the lake, into an area illuminated by bright light.

A couple walking their dog along the boardwalk notice her and run to lift her face out of the water. I watch them drag her to shore, my heart in my throat as I watch the man perform CPR for what feels like hours. Her first gurgled response engulfs me with relief. For the first time since I woke and saw my destroyed body on those train tracks, I felt joy. In fact, I'm not sure when the last time I felt such joy was.

The relief I feel that she's ok is overcome by regret at what I've done. I've brought so much pain to so many people—I wish I could take it away. Suddenly their pain feels more important than the emptiness I had in the time leading up to my death. I wasn't alone, and I wasn't unloved. Every life is interconnected—whatever one does affects the lives of everyone else, even if they can't see it.

My vision is taken by the brightest light I've ever seen and I'm pulled towards it. A sense of calm acceptance spreads through me as I pass into the light. *Who would have thought the old codger was right.* The beginning is over, now it's time to move on.

About the author

Carolyn Young is a single mum living in Melbourne with her children and rescue cats. Most her writing falls under the speculative fiction banner with Young Adult dystopian as her main focus. She has several short stories appearing in both Australian and international publications.

A considerable amount of her life has been spent moving from one university course to another trying to find her place in the world before realising her interest in reading extended to an even stronger passion for writing.

She now spends her spare time reading, writing and dreaming of the day she can move to the country and write full-time.
As a writer she credits any and all success to her cat, who always knows the right keys to walk over to inspire creativity.
Follow Carolyn at https://www.facebook.com/authorcarolynyoung.

Bugles Bred &
Bugles Born

Rebecca Dale

[INTERVIEW2018SEP03.wav]

Look, it wasn't the first time I'd seen a person lose control in a Westfield. Men just aren't built for lattés and the Fresh Food People. Maybe the ladies like shopping around, but it just gets to a man, you know? You have a list of things you need when you go in, then you leave with a trolley full of other things you don't. Crazy. And where you go makes no difference—Chatswood, Hornsby, Burwood—all of them carbon copies, decked out in lino that looks like soggy toast. Don't look too close anyway, mate, because you know that's not discolouration near the bin, that's pure grime and baby vomit. Don't look!

Probably the noise set him off. Fuck! Decibels curling up the walls and spewing down from those domed ceilings like torture itself. Commercial cathedrals, filled to the brim with the chatter of a thousand questions, each more pointed and pointless than the last. Should we get the red or the blue? Can I have a doughnut? Why does he get one and I don't? Jesus Christ, what does it matter if the sheets are Egyptian or not? If old Richie didn't move his store from the old strip on Burdett Street I wouldn't have been there at all. Desperate times.

But it makes you pay attention, a sound like that. My *body* heard it; my shoulders up and hackled right away. Something in that growl rose and lanced across the cavern into the back of my skull until lashings of adrenalin coated my spine. The sort of grunt that you use on a guy at a bar who thinks he can take a piece of you. The family next to me stopped in their tracks. The mother, her voice soft and nervous, reached out and caught her son by the wrist, eyes trained to the corner near the Bing Lee. I slowed and took a bite of my croissant. People need to learn that men just get angry. It's not something to get all emotional about. Cowering like an animal backed into a corner doesn't help anything. Just go about your business. Don't make a spectacle. You stop in groups like that and a man gets self-conscious. Don't poke the bear, for fuck's sake.

Besides, I had a trumpet to pick up. A collection to finally—*finally*—complete.

God, young girls are experts when it comes to a pitiful face, aren't they? As I rounded the corner, there was this kid, barely thirteen, and she had the whole routine down perfect, the tears clinging to her lashes like little glistening dewdrops. Just my luck, she blocked the door to my ticket out of this domestic hellhole. *Richard's Guitar Factory And Other Fine Instruments,* said the sign. So close and yet so far.

When I go to bed these days that's what I see. I see the way she was curled into the shop's glass window, shrinking away from him and nodding her head, shielding the soft parts under her ribcage with her hands. He tore up the air with his voice again and again. *Stop it,* he said. *Stop it, stop it, what's wrong with you,* and every single time she flinched away. When he raised his hand, curled into a fist so tight his knuckles were white against the fluorescent downlights, she sobbed and bellowed. She laid herself down like a marionette doll with cut strings and ruined on the floor.

I don't think he punched her, no matter what anyone said. But I didn't see it, because what I remember most, what I still dream about, is that glimmer of something where her hair tucked behind her ear. Sometimes I wake up sweating, seeing a knife, but that's my dream making it something else. The palms of her hands pushed up against the glass like suction cups, and it was never a blade, but the metallic sheen of the instrument behind her, revealed between the curve of her neck as she contorted away from him. Mate, it was so weird being there and seeing the King Liberty, my King Liberty, behind this fragile creature with the quivering lip. Beautiful, beautiful thing, that trumpet. One of a kind. Even with this whole debacle going on, it was hard not to look at it. Part of me worried she'd break the glass and damage it, which would have been a damn shame because it was mint, polished to the perfect shine. I had to have it. Couldn't get me into a clusterfuck like Westfield for any other reason. Richie's an asshole for not just driving it over. I'm a repeat customer. I would have made it worth his while.

When his fist came down I don't recall it connecting. I didn't hear anything like that, you know? Just her scream. And look, someone would have called the police. A man couldn't beat up a young woman, even his daughter, while everybody watched and did nothing. That shit doesn't happen, no matter what those snowflakes on Twitter say. You should have seen the way people carried on after that, stepping between them and following him with their phones out, recording him. What about civil liberties? Anyway I'm getting ahead of myself. That's not the important bit, the father. But you're the expert on these things, so you tell me.

We need to go back to the moment where the glass quivered. And the girl, she saw it as clearly as I did, like a stone had skipped over the surface and made it ripple. Maybe it was some trick of the light, an effect of pressure and physics. All I know is that her hand was on the glass and I swear, that trumpet wasn't polished metal and valve. It reached for her, like that movie with the sword in the lake. It slipped through the glass and brushed along the back of her neck, no longer an instrument but a hand, old and rusted and whispering. But then the guy was back, never left, never stopped and screamed at her to get up, pulled her to her feet, jerking her along behind him.

Here we go. Of course I didn't do anything because what can you do? If he was hitting her at home I'd only have made it worse. You think the other people made a difference? And no, I don't know what happened before I showed up. Maybe it's an act on her part. Maybe she's a problem child. And the mother was there, right beside him, just watching on as if she was bored, her head down. What does that tell you? Mothers protect their children; maternal instinct. Besides, this kind of thing is private. Look, I'm paying you so keep your judgements to yourself.

I ducked into the store, but not before I caught a glimpse of her face as he dragged her away. She looked back like that King

Liberty was the centre of her world. I thought I was the only one who looked at brass like that. Inside, the shelves and shop fittings dulled the sound and it was easier to forget about it. I had to wave my hands in Richie's face to snap him out of it, but I think he was glad to make a sale so quickly. He brought out the case from the back, its innards were worn velvet. The glass cabinet clinked as he turned the key and took out my prize.

I held the instrument in my hands. This was the time-honoured ritual. I brought the mouthpiece to my lips, pursing them into the correct position and blasted a single stream of air. The metal was ice cold, enough to make me shiver. A sound ruptured out and I swear I'm not making this up—it was exactly the measure and shape of her whimper, a strange and strangled thing. Funny huh? And when I took it to the counter, there was this tension, the feeling of an elastic band where my hands touched the valves, like it could slip out of my fingers at any moment. It tried to pull away from me, this prize of mine, somewhere into the distance beyond me. But I held it tight. I paid for that silver-plated beauty. It's mine.

Even as I hold it now, I feel that pulling all the way down to my bones. How do you explain that, genius?

⸙

[VOICEMAIL__14SEP[4].mp3]

Answer the phone, woman!

I got your email and I think you're full of shit. How many times do I need to tell you this isn't about the girl? Anyway I did what you said. I went to the police and they were just as ho-hum as I was. Apparently there's this law about parents and children. You know, to deal with smacks and other light offences. Maybe the guy overstretched that day, but maybe he didn't. No-one called the cops. You have to remember that. If she was in trouble, it's everyone's fault, not just mine. Anyway, he took my number but says there's not much they can do, particularly when it happened over a week ago. I'm the one who's suffering now. Can't you do some spell and make all this go away? I'll pay for it. Money is not a problem here.

Richie turned up at my house. I always know it's him because he rings the buzzer three times. Brought me pad thai and a six pack. He left it at the door when he realised I wasn't going to answer. The walls and windows muffled whatever he said. Maybe he thought I cared about his opinions because he wrote *I'm worried about you* onto a scrap of paper and taped it to the plastic tub. But I just want to sleep. I want to close my eyes and not be afraid.

That's why you've gotta help me. I don't even recognise my own voice anymore. It sounds like one of those squeaky dog toys that's been chewed to bits. There's still incense and musk clinging to my tablecloth from your visit yesterday and now I can't even drink a cup of tea without inhaling it. I don't even like tea. I am not into this weird new age shit. I am not this person, who goes to some crazy psychic witch doctor because of a few bad dreams.

I'm sorry, *karmic therapist*. Is that what you said?

You know, this pad thai isn't bad, even if it is cold.

I know you said not to play it, but I can't help it. That's the only thing I can do to keep the damn thing here. Every night I put it in its original case, just like you said, inside its own display column. Not even thin air should be able to get in, and I've put three damn locks on it. That shit is archival quality. But every morning it's the same. Bad dreams and the trumpet at the front door. Nightmares of hands and valves and the sound of her whimper. Every morning when I pick it up, it's so cold it feels like it could burn. And then I play, because it's a beautiful instrument. Great timbre. There's strength and earth and longing in it. The kind of instrument that moves mountains. This is the bugle before war. I looked for it for so long. It cost me a fortune. I shouldn't have to give it up.

You don't know how hard it was to complete my collection. I have one of every King trumpet ever made. I travelled across the world to furnish this little room. On a good afternoon when the sun filters through the stain-worked glass—this is a Federation cottage, almost a hundred years old so the glass is thick, the best quality—a kaleidoscope of colour slips over the spoils of my labours. The silversonic I got in New Orleans. The one-piece I haggled over in Hong Kong.

I don't care what you say. I'm not leaving the door open. Ever. It doesn't belong to her. Shit, I have to go. I think I'm going to throw up.

[VOICEMAIL__19SEP(COPY).mp3]

Why don't you answer the phone? I sent you more money.

Do you really think I could have done anything? Look, it's hard to be a man, alright? Sometimes you lose control. Women test you. First they want you to do everything; make the money, make all the fucking decisions, and then when you don't get it right they come after you. Sometimes you just need to do some-thing to get your piece. I know he didn't stop and he should have. But that man deserves forgiveness the same as anyone else. Sometimes we do things that we're not proud of. He's her dad, he loves her. Fathers love their daughters, their sons. Besides, why doesn't she go to the police if it's so bad? And what about her mother? She just stood there like a ghost, not even a glimmer of life on her face, watching the whole thing. It's her job, right?

There's nothing I could have done for her. Of course it's monstrous, what happened. But that girl will get out someday. I am not obligated.

I need you to explore other options. Giving up the Liberty is not an option. Okay bye.

[NSWPOLICES20457899 - Single handwritten note on kitchen table]

The trumpet is a troubadour's instrument. In the olden days, wherever their hearts would take them, minstrels went from town to town across Europe, bartering their songs and souls for coin. The trumpet was born in those days. You can always play a horn, even if it's rusted and wilted. Lightweight. Put it in your pack and get out of there. Off to the next port.

That's what I thought when I held my first brass, some Yamaha thing my mother bought me in my primary school days. I played the first note and knew what love was. Not the love of fairytales, but the love of a champion, bettering his songs to win the heart and mind of a damsel who would never spare him a glance. And when you failed, and the men with swords and gleaming helms came for you, you moved on.

Trumpets are freedom. There isn't a single soul that's played one and felt anything but contentment.

[VOICEMAIL_20SEP.MP3]

I swear it's not the same girl. It couldn't be. Please, if there was a time to pick up it's right now. Are you there?

I can hear her through the door. Her voice is so steady it makes the knot in my stomach explode. I've told her already that it's not hers. But she just keeps saying open up, open up. Can you hear that? I'll put the phone to the door. It doesn't sound like her. There's a sac of liquid fear under my lungs, spreading through my body. I want to scream. No, not happening. Just a girl. And I'm a man. She's the one who should be afraid. Not me. How did she even find me?

That pull, again. God, it's so strong it takes everything in my soul to hold onto it. She can't have my King Liberty. Not this one! Shit! Do you hear the knocking? This wouldn't be happening if I wasn't so weak. I haven't eaten. I haven't slept. But I'll hurt her if she dares to come in. This trumpet is mine! I'm bringing it to my lips right now. Maybe it will scare her off. I'm the one who bought it. I'm the one that polished it. I'm the one who plays it. Not her. Listen, witch, you'd better come for me when you hear this.

Why am I shivering? My breath is ghosting in the air, it's so cold. Okay, okay, okay. This thing, whatever it is, that beats and breathes, that's metal and valves, this alive thing, it wants to be with her. But that's not right. I paid. I minded my business. I'm a good person. I pay my taxes. I go to church every Easter.

Just let me play it one last time.

[VOICEMAIL_20SEP(2-FINAL).mp3]

I'm sorry, I dropped the phone.

She was a whole different person. Tall and strong but not in the way that bodies are. First just a silhouette against the setting sun. I didn't open the door, or did I? It's so blurry. I saw the fingers out of the corner of my eye. I heard the mechanism of the lock, metal on metal, clunking into place. The wood creaked beneath the shining fingertips. I looked up and there she was, eyes clear and piercing into my soul. Whatever fibers were left in my carcass—rotting and fragile—came apart under that gaze. A kind voice, soft, soothing. She didn't tell me things were going to be okay because they weren't. In that last moment, I thought the elastic between her and my King Liberty would cut me into two pieces. Pressure on both sides of my face, clawing into my eye sockets as I opened my mouth to scream, and then... nothing. Lightness, weakness. I want to sleep for days. I want to never wake up and forget that all of this happened.

I'll never forget the shadow of the instrument, cutting out the light as she raised it, and then the sound, bright and pure enough to make angels weep. Her fingers wrapped expertly around the valves as the pitch wavered, the most sophisticated tremolo I've ever heard and I would have cried if I had the energy. But there's nothing left in the empty shape of who I was. I was so afraid, because God help me if she wanted to end me, to take revenge. But I don't exist wherever she's going. Once I was hindrance and pain and now I am nothing.

Her laughter was as bright as her bugle; there were reams of it as the melody ended and she began, pouring into the cicada song, insects piled into the trees outside, their exoskeletons littered on the cracked pavement. They crunched under her foot as she left. I don't know where she's going, but it's not backwards, it's not homewards. Nobody with a song like that is going home.

About the author:

Rebecca Dale is a writer and librarian. She studied ancient history and archaeology at the University of Sydney before pursuing a masters in Applied Linguistics and a graduate diploma in Library and Information Services. For the last ten years she has been working in public and academic libraries, producing copy for library training, marketing, exhibitions and community engagement. Her last publication was "The new librarian's roadmap: at the crossroads of expectation and reality" for the Australian Library Journal. She lives in Sydney with a very adorable and mischievous rabbit. You can follow her on Instagram (IG: @ladygreysydney) or at her website www.rebeccadale.com.au.

Dealt in Sin

Sasha Hanton

THE HEADY SMELL OF lavender choked the air. Shadows danced across the walls, twisting with the flicker of candlelight. Morgan sat in the centre of the room, her burgundy hair tumbling over her shoulders and creating a veil over her face.

She had agonised over every little detail in her preparation and it had taken days of planning to acquire the resources for the ritual. The thick white chalk lines alone had taken over a day to correctly mark on the cement floor. Twisted words rolled off her tongue as she started with a whisper, slowly raising her voice. Her eyes were closed, the strain of keeping them that way but a small price to pay if this worked. She felt a breeze surrounding her, heard the low whistle piercing the silence and sensed—deep in her gut—the pull of magic, fear and anxiousness.

"Who summons me?" The voice assailed her ears, its words creeping inside her and writhing beneath her skin. Biting her bottom lip and clenching her nails into her palms, Morgan struggled to keep her eyes closed.

"I, Morgan Elway, summon you." Her teeth clamped to her lip as she muttered the words; no matter what she couldn't let her guard down.

"Why?" A shiver travelled the length of Morgan's spine as the singular word ricocheted back and forth in her brain.

"I seek a deal." There was a throbbing pain in her lip but she dared not allow herself to open her mouth. A sickly wet smacking sound filled the room, and it took all her focus to keep her eyes from springing open.

"How delicious," another smacking sound echoed out, "and what pray tell are you seeking?"

"I need a flock, a coven if you will." Morgan was sick of being alone, the lone practitioner in her humble town. Pushing through the growing strain and pain she held onto her goal; to have more witches join her.

"And what will you pay for this?"

"My soul, anything I can grant which you desire."

"Very well, so shall it be."

EBONY HAD BEEN DRAWN to the small town. She wasn't sure why, she just knew that it called to her. She hadn't been practising long when she saw an advertisement for the town. She instantly knew she had to go there, that if she did she would find sisterhood.

It hadn't taken long for her to find Morgan, it was almost as if fate was guiding them together. The head of the local coven wasn't overly charismatic or intimidating but there was this radiance to her aura, and none of the other witches in the coven ever questioned her leadership.

Ebony could feel it in her bones as soon as she'd met Morgan, that this was where she was meant to be. It consumed her every waking moment, she went from dabbling in magic to a fully practising witch in a blink of the eye. After months in Morgan's presence Ebony found herself in love with her new home, her new sisters, but most of all, her mistress.

Imitating Morgan, looking and acting like Morgan, became all Ebony could think about. She despised her flat ashy blonde hair and craved Morgan's rich burgundy waves. It was odd how compelled she felt to copy her mistress.

Ebony found it impossible to fight the urge, she wanted, no, needed to do something to make herself more like Morgan. So she snuck her way into her leader's home determined to steal a hair from Morgan's comb, then she could perform the ritual to transform her own hair into Morgan's, to make her the same as Morgan. A simple plan it was not, and what was worse is Ebony found herself privy to secrets she did not want to know. In her mind it had been so consuming, her need to get the hair, that it didn't matter if Morgan caught her because she would handle that obstacle if it came up.

Finding the comb had been easy, the jeweled exterior sparkled and reflected even the smallest hint of light on the top of Morgan's dresser. Elated with herself Ebony had giggled in glee as she ran her fingers gently across the fine teeth to pluck out Morgan's hair. In her euphoria she hadn't heard the jingle of keys or the sound of the front door opening, no she hadn't heard anything until the thick thud of footsteps on floorboards. Morgan was home and Ebony was still here, she would be furious if she found Ebony here. There was only one option, Ebony had to hide but where? Her eyes flickered across the room frantically until they alighted on a set of thick maple doors.

Ebony found herself hidden away in the cupboard as Morgan entered her abode. She found herself gazing through a gap between the doors as Morgan disrobed, and muffled a shriek at the sight of twisting burn marks across Morgan's skin. She felt her stomach twisting into knots, this was a demonic contract.

As her eyes beheld the contract, a fog lifted from her mind. The all-consuming desire to copy Morgan evaporated and she was left with a horrifying revelation. All Morgan's powers, the way that she and others had been drawn to the coven, it was all from some twisted deal with a demon. Ebony felt like she was going to be sick, but choked back her feelings and remained hidden until Morgan left. She fled from Morgan's home, not even sure where she was running to.

COBWEBS AND DUST OCCUPIED almost every corner of the church, the pews had been vacant for a long time. Still, Father Thomas insisted on keeping it open for any who might seek comfort.

The confessional was run down and some of the wood had started to rot, but Father Thomas insisted on sitting and waiting to hear confessions at least twice a day. Nobody ever came, except for the odd case once or twice a year. The town had long since slipped into sin, possibly past the point of salvation, though he would still stay and do the Lord's work when possible.

On that crisp, winter day Father Thomas sat, hoping that someone would come, yet expecting another uninterrupted day. Seated inside the confessional with a thermos of tea, he jumped when he heard the tell-tale creak of the church door opening, almost did a spit take when he heard the soft lilting sounds of a feminine voice express the common words for starting a confession.

"Forgive me, Father, for I have sinned."

"How have you sinned, my child?"

"I have unwittingly been in service of a demon, Father."

"Well, that's... did you say demon?"

"Yes, I don't know what demon it was, but as soon as I discovered it I came right here. I don't know what to do Father," cried the voice.

"And how did you find yourself in the demon's service?" Usually in confessional Father Thomas wouldn't pry for further details but the mention of demons had his interest piqued.

"I'm not sure, I only moved here not long ago... perhaps that was by the demon's designs too. I felt... drawn here."

Father Thomas hummed in acknowledgement, not wanting to interrupt.

"I practice witchcraft Father, I know it's a sin but I don't practice it maliciously."

"A sin is still a sin, my child."

"Yes, of course, I'll stop practising I promise. I don't honestly think I can continue to after what I've seen, a fellow witch who I practice with... the head of our coven actually, she's the one who made a deal with the demon." A choked sob came through the partition. "How could she do such a thing, Father?"

"The devil has many ways of tempting people from God's path, my child. Though I cannot say what would have driven your friend to deal with a demon."

"I can't believe Morgan would do this, it taints everything—"

Morgan, the name sent a shock straight through Father Thomas—Morgan Elway. A social outcast in the town, a dour girl who always kept to herself and was always wearing black, her mother had been a faithful member of the church years ago but Morgan had never seemed to enjoy it.

"Father, please tell me what I should do? Is there some way to cleanse myself after my dealings with her?"

"Uh, yes, of course, cleansing yourself is a priority. Are you baptised, my child?" Snapped from his thoughts Thomas returned to the task at hand.

"Yes, I am baptised."

"Good, then I should think nightly prayers to the Lord and a series of Hail Mary's should do the trick. And child, you must distance yourself as far away from Morgan and her demon bargain as possible."

"Thank you, Father." After a few moments the tell-tale sound of the church door signaled that whoever it was, had left.

Overnight, Father Thomas was tortured by the knowledge of Morgan's demonic dealings, as a man of the cloth it disturbed him deeply. His dreams were filled with fire and brimstone—the town he called home collapsing around him enslaved by some terrible demon. At the centre of it all was Morgan Elway.

Awakened in a cold sweat, he knew there would be no saving the people of his town if Morgan was left unchecked. A slippery slope of thoughts presented themselves to him, no matter how he tried his reasoning had already slipped so far down that there was only one answer he could come upon. *'Thou shalt not suffer a witch to live.'* The longer he thought on the matter the more his mind nagged. *'You cannot drink the cup of the Lord and the cup of demons too; you cannot have a part in both the Lord's table and the table of demons.'*

Verses from scripture whispered into his mind, he found himself acting as if on auto pilot. Leaving the church unattended, he drove himself to Morgan's house. Finding the door unlocked, he headed inside. Her house was a den of sin, and as he entered each new room Father Thomas crossed himself.

"What are you doing here?"

The shocked voice startled him, and he turned to see Morgan in the hallway.

"Father Thomas, what are you doing here?"

It happened in a blur, he barely noticed he had done it until it was over. A ceremonial dagger that had been on a side table now dripped crimson red, and Morgan's body lay limp on the floor. Another verse from scripture rang out through his mind as he stood there, bewildered at what he had done. *For our struggle is not against flesh and blood, but against the rulers, against the authorities, against the powers of this dark world and against the spiritual forces of evil in the heavenly realms.'* He crumpled to the floor, a sob escaping him, for he could not tell if he had done the Lord's work, or the Devil's.

PAIN, RIPPLING CRUSHING pain spread all through her body. Everything burned, every sense she had was overwhelmed with scorching heat. Her lungs felt as if they were on fire, yet at the same time as if they were filled with fluid.

"Ugh," she coughed and spluttered, emerging into consciousness. Bleary-eyed she couldn't recognise her surroundings, and that all-encompassing pain still ravaged her body. "Oh hell."

As her vision cleared it became apparent she was no longer on the mortal plane. The thick, swirling clouds of smoke that wafted all around and the raging fires that burnt near her made that extremely evident.

"Welcome, Morgan Elway." A shiver ran down her spine, as a familiar terrifying voice wormed its way under her skin.

"Where am I?" She twisted left and right, trying to catch sight of the demon. As she moved, the reason for the mixed sensations in her lungs became apparent, she stood in knee-deep fiery liquid.

"The Lake of Fire, though I should hope that is fairly evident." The voice snaked around her, coming from every direction at once.

"Why?"

The demon chuckled. "Because you promised your soul to me."

"I mean, how? What happened to me?" Her memory was hazy, all of it a muddled mess.

"Doesn't matter how, you died and now your soul is mine." There was a bite to the voice, and the words caused her skin to sting. "Now hurry up out of there."

Morgan's body felt sluggish as she waded through the liquid and scorching flames. Her body felt as if she was being ripped apart, as if the flesh would fall from her bones. And yet she emerged from the Lake of Fire unmarred.

"Where are you?" On the banks of the lake, she still could not see any physical signs of the demon.

"All around you, Morgan Elway." The thick clouds of smoke curled and encircled her.

"Oh," Morgan gulped as the smoke twisted into a humanoid form.

"And now that I've collected on our deal, I've got a special job for you."

"A job?" It's a bit like looking a gift horse in the mouth, Morgan supposed as the question left her mouth. "I just, I thought it'd be eternal damnation and torture."

A cackle burst forth from the smoke, the figure dispersed and then reformed.

"Oh no, that would be too easy. Hardly a fair trade for what I gave you." The words made Morgan's skin crawl. "What I want is for you to work for me. You'll spend eternity serving me by collecting souls."

"That hardly seems fair; I only reaped the benefits of our deal for a short time!" cried Morgan.

"Tsk, tsk, a deal is still a deal!" As the demon roared out those words heavy chains appeared. Morgan found herself on a horse, her hands bound to the reins. "Now ride. Enjoy your new life as a soul collector!"

The horse took off at the demon's command, starting at a light trot, then breaking into a lightning-paced gallop. Her hands bound to the reins, Morgan leaned forward and strained to keep herself in the saddle, her eyes shut tight against the wind.

When the horse slowed from its frantic pace, her eyes opened and she was shocked to find herself at the outskirts of her hometown. Her eyes traced the outlines of familiar buildings, longing heavy in her chest. A burning, tingling sensation built up beneath her skin until a white-hot heat seemed to sear her vision. She managed to keep herself in the saddle as the pain caused her to bite into her lip with muffled screams of agony until it subsided.

When the pain ebbed away, she blinked her eyes repeatedly until her vision cleared. Morgan frowned when she realised that all sense of colour had escaped her. Expect for one vivid speck of orange off in the distance that seemed to irritate her retinas, it was as if she was living in an old movie of varying shades of grey.

There was no manual to explain what she should do, no supervisor to ask about this predicament, only her and the horse. Her steed exhaled loudly, wisps of thick smoke filled the air, as it stomped the ground in impatience. With the change in her sight and no clue on how to proceed Morgan could see only one option, ride for the speck of orange.

Riding through the streets Morgan passed no one and heard nothing but the wind. As she drew closer the speck flared into a bright fiery mass, until its colour practically overwhelmed her.

At the centre of the colour stood a figure, the first sign of life since Morgan had entered the town. Her eyes focused on the person before her, and she was filled with clarity. They stood in the dusty old church, the figure before them kneeling deep in prayer. The chains upon Morgan's hands unwound themselves from the reins and morphed into a whip.

A RESOUNDING BOOM OF thunder filled the air, shaking the walls of the church and setting Father Thomas' heart racing. Still, he kept praying, hoping somehow God would tell him he was forgiven. Another rumbling sounded overhead, jostling him from his prayers.

He opened his eyes, turned his gaze upwards and sought out heaven amongst the cobwebs as a third thunderous clap rung out. A surge of lightning pierced the weak timber, causing the rotted wood to collapse and rain down on the priest.

As he drew a final breath from beneath the debris a figure appeared before him. He dared to hope for salvation but instead, was faced with utter devastation. When the thunder bellowed for the fourth time, it was accompanied by the distinct crack of a whip and the sting of cord biting into skin. He was yanked from the debris, but his mortal body was left behind. His sins had come for him.

ABOUT THE AUTHOR

Sasha Hanton grew up in the tropics of Darwin, Northern Territory. From a young age, she devoured books and iced coffee, both of which she continues to intake on an almost daily basis. Now living on beautiful Bribie Island in Queensland her time is split between writing and spoiling her canine companion Molly.

Sasha, who has a Bachelor of Journalism from Bond University, has dabbled in the journalistic profession but finds fiction far more fascinating. Her first published work The Short Story Press Collection draws on her love for a diverse range of genres and passion for short stories.

Throughout her life, she has been a lover of history and mythology, and at any time will find some way to worm one or the other into her storytelling. When she's not writing or reading she can be found tending to her garden or fostering dogs in need. You can keep up with her writing over on www.theshortstorypress.wordpress.com

THANK YOU FOR READING! If you enjoyed Beginnings, please consider leaving a review.

About Aussie Speculative Fiction: We are a community of Australian readers and writers of speculative fiction, particularly aimed at supporting Indie writers.

www.aussiespeculativefiction.com